O HOLY HECK

KATHLEEN PENDOLEY

Kathleen Pendoley
AUTHOR

For this life

1

*S*now, cold enough to be ice, nicks my cheeks and forces my eyes shut as I push the door open with my hip, bracing myself against the resistance. The wind bites hard, whipping my hair into my mouth. Frigid air blows inside the hall, pushing flakes far within before they melt.

Brumal Heights hasn't had a storm of this caliber in years.

Gone is the snug feeling from when I curled up on the sofa. Gazing back wistfully, a mug of hot chocolate and a bowl of buttered popcorn taunt me from the side table where I left them to tide me over as I watched a movie and waited for the roast beef to finish cooking. Best laid plans…

"Hurry up, Craig." Blinded by blowing ice shards, I grab a stiff canvas sleeve and yank him inside. Enough snow covers the fabric to make a decent-sized snowball. Wrapping my fist around ice that burns like fire, I conceal the weapon behind my back. Whoa to the person who interrupts my holiday cheer.

"Cool your jets, Faith. I'm here to help." The gorilla-sized man shakes his way out of his excessive garb, adding a layer of snow onto the carpet.

My face speaks volumes. "Cool my j—"

He cuts me off. "Come see," Craig exclaims, voice eager like a kid on Christmas morning. He grabs my arm and guides me toward the window, nudging me along while kicking the door closed with his boot. The shriek of wind dies at once, replaced by Craig's shrill soprano as I sneak behind him and drop the snowball down his back.

"Ugh! Like I'm not already freezing after plowing the mall parking lot and shoveling all the walkways at the senior center."

"You've got a heart of gold, my friend." I pick up my now lukewarm cocoa and hand it to him.

He gulps down half and licks away a chocolate mustache. "Mmm. Is that caramel in there?"

"My secret recipe." I don't mention that it's a cheat. Just pour warm milk over Swiss Miss cocoa and Werther's Candy to taste. Let the brew rest for a few minutes until it reaches a temperature that won't scald the tongue.

Draining the last drops, Craig puts the mug beside the popcorn and grabs a handful. Crunching, he motions to the window. Snow blasts outside, whipping into a cyclone and creating a whiteout. Experts predict twelve to eighteen inches before the storm eases. Unless it changes course as it spins over the coast, Christmas will be canceled. I won't be the only one spending the holidays alone. Not just the day—the whole season is mine. Is there a better phrase than "winter break"? I doubt it.

The storm has all the makings of a typical Nor'easter— long, drawn out, and damaging. With the snow drifts so high, it's hard to see where my yard ends and the street begins. At least the trees are still standing, for now.

"What exactly am I looking at?" I ask.

"The driveway." Using his meaty paws, he swivels my

head to the right. I feel a satisfying pop in my neck, releasing the pinched vertebrae that have ached since I fell off my bike a year ago. The force surprises me, but the relief quickly outweighs any annoyance.

"Ahh." My sigh sounds racier than intended, but he doesn't bat an eye. He's still looking for praise for clearing my SUV and driveway.

"Impressive. Thank you." I don't mention how fifteen minutes will have it covered and buried as deeply as when he arrived. A good deed is a good deed.

Craig crosses his arms over his broad chest. Proudly dressed in a dark gray uniform of his own design, the gray embroidered tag over his left pec reads Craig's Towing on the top and Craig Bennett, Owner and Operator, beneath. The mirror hanging on the wall behind him reflects the back, a picture of his black and chrome tow truck and Craig's Towing slogan, "We'll getcha going."

One of my favorite past students—I allow the colloqui-alism for catchiness. Since he graduated, Craig stops by every few weeks to help with chores I can't or don't have time to do, such as landscaping, snow removal, or projects that require power tools. As a founder and teacher at Divergent Academy, a Montessori-style school, I find nothing more fulfilling than witnessing the impact of alternative education. Our graduates aren't rocket scientists or college professors, but we send many entrepreneurs and loyal employees into the world.

"Do you think you're jumping the gun? We've hours yet for the storm to reach its peak, let alone pass through."

"You gotta keep up," he explains. "The plow hasn't been out in a year, and I can't get stuck. I'm the tow truck driver, too. It gets harder to switch between vehicles as the tempera-ture drops, and people get antsy enough to try their hand at driving in a storm. Plus, I got no problem coming back and doing it again."

"Have no problem," I correct him.

"Aww, come on, Teach. I done gradeeated."

I smack his shoulder without force. "Grammar matters, bub. Now, I'm sensing an ulterior motive for this visit. Let me guess. Are you hungry? Is it time for dinner, or will a hearty snack suffice?"

He rubs his slight paunch and admits, "I could eat. Snack, meal, buffet. Long nights like tonight burn up plenty of calories."

"You got it. Follow me."

My two-hundred-year-old house is tiny. Just five strides and you're in the kitchen. My Dad likes to say he has to go outside to change his mind. Dads and their jokes! But I love the coziness. It's so rustic and small that firewood keeps it heated through fall and winter. The stone fireplace opens to both the living room and bedroom. A smaller brick fireplace, added around 1930, warms the kitchen and bathroom. The front room and mudroom aren't wired to the furnace or have fireplaces, so a ceramic space heater follows me when needed. Old-growth trees help keep the house cool during warmer months, provided the windows remain open.

As a single woman, messes aren't an issue. With a living space that aspires to hit one thousand square feet, it wouldn't matter if they did. Cleaning is a cinch. Upkeep, especially with Craig's dirt-cheap prices, is affordable. So, yeah. People can have their big houses. They're beautiful, but upgrading my simple space would require an extraordinary sales pitch.

Craig grabs two glasses from the cabinet and fills them with tap water before sitting at the table, as is his habit when we break bread. He claims I'm a better cook than his mother and saves his appetite whenever I'm on the rounds roster. I enjoy experimenting with flavors and appreciate his willing-ness to be my guinea pig.

I pull a glistening roast from the oven, using bear paw mitts. My mouth waters, but the thermometer indicates that thirty minutes remain. I add the boiled potatoes to the roasting pan with the juices, return them to the oven, and set the timer. Then I gather quick supplies for a cheese and veggie tray.

"Sorry. I wasn't prepared for guests. I'll have to nuke the brie."

He gasps and clutches at his chest. "Is this how you treat all your guests or only the special ones?"

"Quitcha bitchin' and tell me something good."

His head rears back in surprise at my bastardization of the language.

"Teachers can tease, too," I quip.

After filling a small plate for myself, I push the dish, still piled high with cheese, crackers, green grapes, carrot sticks, and almonds, in front of Craig. He'll finish it without a problem.

We catch up on our lives since our last dinner chat. Craig always has a story about the calls that come in, often funny, sometimes tragic, usually happening after midnight. Today, he shares how a twelve-year-old girl stole her parents' BMW to buy makeup that they had forbidden her to wear. She rammed into the giant oak tree owned by the neighbors across the street. The misconception young people have about how little movement is needed to steer was her Achilles' heel. The vehicle spun around before coming to a jarring stop, taking out the front end of the shiny vehicle. Besides being grounded for the rest of her natural life, the girl walked away without injury.

I updated him on Jeff Hanson, a student with whom I've

been having the most trouble this year. The six-year-old boy continues to struggle with fine motor skills and maintaining eye contact, despite my one-on-one work with him throughout the semester.

"I know he has it in him to excel someday. Right now, it's just a gut feeling. But it's like his real self is locked in there. It's all about finding the right key."

My story hits close to home.

"If anyone can get to the heart of him, it's you, Teach. Your student just turned six. I was, what? Eleven before I smartened up."

"It's not so much the age as the time it's taking. You turned around on day one, right after you learned the importance of playing by the rules."

Craig fell hard. He blushes crimson at the reminder of his first crush.

Humans are vulnerable, especially during puberty. Wearing your heart on your sleeve is dangerous, and I took seriously the responsibility of receiving those fears, desires, and hormones. I used firm boundaries and gentle let-downs to prevent him from getting hurt. To be honest, Craig finding me irresistible helped him come out of his shell. Labeled "trouble" at his last school, Craig won a lottery spot at Divergent Academy the year we were accredited. When I walked into homeroom, he was pulling the hair of a chubby, moon-faced girl, tears streaming down her face. He had also cornered a pale, freckle-faced boy and threatened him with the same.

I recount when I sidled up, catching him unawares, and said, "Say you look like a take-charge kind of guy. Would you like to be my class partner?"

His eyes roamed my face and then, in that untamed pubescent male way, lower. His head jerked back, and his eyes dilated as he appreciated our differences.

"Eyes on mine."

He stopped gaping and looked up with a blush on his cheeks. Then, without prompting, let go of the girl's hair and allowed the boy to flee his prison.

I gathered both of the victims close and sat on a nearby chair.

"Let's go over the rules. The most important thing is that the class partner must be trusted by their fellow students. Do you think Celia and Devin trust you right now?"

Celia sat in my lap, chest hitching as her tears slowed.

I rocked her gently and pointed to a box of tissues on my desk.

Craig paused before catching my drift, plucking a few tissues, and handing them to Celia. She dried her face and blew her nose with a jarring "honk."

"What would you like to say to Celia?"

"I'm sorry. You can trust me now."

"And?"

"And I won't pull your hair again."

"What else do you need from Craig, Celia?" I asked.

She rubbed her face against my chest, eyes squeezed shut.

"Okay. We'll give you a minute."

I turned my attention to Devin, tucked beneath my arm. "How about you, honey? What do you need?"

All our students must be communicative to attend Divergent Academy. They don't have to be Shakespeare, but simple sentences like "I'm hungry" and "I need to potty" are necessary. Devin can speak, but chooses not to.

"Well, it's tough using our words sometimes, isn't it?"

Devin's head bobbed up and down so fast I almost missed it.

Celia released a shuddering sigh.

"How about we start with an apology?"

"Sorry," Craig repeated, with as little inflection as before. "I won't scare you again."

Devin looked unsure but met Craig's fist in a pardoning bump.

"Way to go, boys. How about we all sing the friendship song?" I motioned to my teaching assistant to gather the rest of the students together. "Let's make a circle around the room," I suggested as I stood and placed Celia on her feet.

It was bedlam for a few minutes as everyone scrambled to find a space.

"You don't have to participate, but friendships grow faster when we hold hands." I reach out my hands to see who will catch them. Craig grabs my left, and Devin holds my right. Craig looks beyond me at the smaller student, offended, glaring at the boy he just apologized to.

"Don't forget the rule, Class Partner," I reminded him.

With a final sneer at Devin, he looked up at me, all innocence and light. "Sorry. I forgot."

I squeezed his hand and said, "Let's work on that."

A dejected Celia opted to remain alone and curled up on a cushion behind me. Before we began, I released the boy's hands and tucked a small teddy bear into her arms. She closed her eyes, and I knew she'd be asleep before the song was through. Being bullied on the first day was a stressful way to start the school year.

Craig turned out to be a terrific advocate. The students trusted him so much that they would share their insecurities and woes with him before anyone else. You wouldn't recognize the engaging man joking, laughing, and eating beside me now as the boy perceived by his public school teachers as one of many who would fall through the cracks.

I shake my head and beam, watching as he carves the roast.

"What?" he asks.

"I'm proud of you, my friend." I raise my glass and propose a toast. "To my first honest-to-goodness success story. The world is a better place since you hung up the bully part of your personality, Mr. Bennett."

He clinks his glass to mine with a humble head tilt.

2

---

*C*raig helps clean the dinner dishes before noticing the time. He pulls on his heavy canvas coat and adjusts a woolen cap to fit low over his forehead and ears.

I hand him a brown bag stuffed with roast beef sandwiches, chips, and fruit to keep him going into the morning.

"Thanks. This'll hit the spot after midnight."

"Text me a thumbs up if you're too busy to write, and let me know how things are going. Feel free to stop by for more food. Remember to get out somewhere safe and walk around every hour or two, or at least when you switch vehicles. It'll keep the blood moving and help you stay awake. I worry about you all alone out there in the dark."

He rejects my fears. "I'm higher up than anyone on the road. None can touch me."

The abrupt and jarring screech of metal outside interrupts our conversation, sharply contradicting his assessment.

"Shit!" Craig laments as we run to the window and peer out. "Someone just hit my truck."

I stifle a giggle at the irony when I see smoke billowing

from underneath the hood of a dark-colored sedan crumpled up behind the tow truck.

"Sounds like he cracked his cooling system. Hear that hissing sound?"

"I can't hear anything over the wind, but you've got a keener ear than I. We'd better check on the driver." I wrap a scarf around my neck and pull on knee-high boots. Following Craig, I head down the driveway.

The man behind the wheel is throwing a fit, punching the steering wheel, and yelling obscenities. He doesn't see us until Craig taps a knuckle on the passenger-side door.

"You okay there, buddy?" Craig calls through the glass. In a quieter voice, he tells me, "Stay behind me. He looks nuts."

I grab onto Craig's arm and peer around it before recognizing the fuming man: Aaron Hanson, Jeff's uncle, the student I'd mentioned over dinner. Jeff's mom, Rachel, is an engaging lady whom I rarely see, while Aaron is the definition of recalcitrant. Isn't that just the way?

The siblings live with Jeff in the behemoth house section of town. Aaron was the architect, but he's a graphic designer by trade. Word is, he had to bail on his dreams when his life imploded around him. The details on that are shady, much like the darkly furrowed brow I'm met with most times we engage. Even I have to admit he did an incredible job directing the build. Floor-to-ceiling windows, wide pocket doors, and handcrafted molding blend walls and ceilings, making the home open and inviting. Antique, comfortable furniture adds a Newport, Rhode Island, cottage feel to the suburban mansion.

According to their neighbors, Aaron and Rachel keep to themselves and are seen as being on the snobbish end of the relatability spectrum. Not one for gossip, I disregard rumors and form my own conclusions about people I don't know. And, based on his barely civil greetings, monosyllabic answers to all questions, unless he's doing the asking, and inability to lighten up, even when Jeff has done something cuter than cute, and all-around chronic cold shoulder condition, I've empirically ascertained that Aaron is, in fact, a snob. Rachel is more shy than snooty, though they complement each other physically. Tall, with black hair and blue eyes, they share a cool countenance that separates them from the rest of us. Rachel will stop and talk to me, whereas Aaron doesn't consider me worthy of conversation unless he's grilling me for entertainment.

Even now, as we try to help, Aaron won't acknowledge us. He's busy using his head as a battering ram against the steering wheel, lips pulled back in a feral grimace.

I don't need this sort of hassle. Not tonight.

I elbow Craig in the side. "Good thing there's a tow truck available, huh? Aaron lives at 1038 Sycamore Street. You've seen it. The house is set back behind an expansive lawn and a driveway lined with dogwood trees that flower in the spring. Drop him off at the end. I'm sure he'll find his way from there."

Craig is all business as he dashes my hopes. "Not tonight. Plowing is the priority. Governor's orders: Emergency tows only until the bulk of the snow falls. No passengers. I'm running late!" He's becoming more worked up by the minute.

My shoulders slump as I glare at Aaron, frustrated by how he's now ruining my free time on top of making my job somewhat awkward and uncomfortable. Things go from bad to worse when I notice his cheeks look wet.

"Is that blood?" I ask Craig.

The sun fell as we ate dinner, so whatever sunshine filtered through the snow was gone. The street has no public lights, and the one that hangs by the door doesn't cast a wide enough beam.

"If it's blood, you have to clean it up. Gas, oil, and wind-shield washer fluid. Those are the liquids I can handle." Craig's voice is high-pitched and thin.

Right. Bodily fluids make Craig feel faint.

"I got this." I push past him and pound on the window. Enough of this foolishness. "Aaron. It's me. Faith."

He freezes, fists raised and prepared to resume his assault on the wheel.

"You're okay, but you're bleeding. Can you come inside so we can assess the damage?"

Typical Aaron, refusing to be civil. He holds still as if that will prevent us from engaging.

Craig looks down at me. "The snow is falling faster. I gotta get outta here and start plowing. I'll push his car behind yours, and then I gotta go."

"Can't he go with you?" I make one more desperate plea, not wanting to be alone with Jeff's uncle. It's awkward enough when Jeff is around as a buffer. Aaron's unpredictable moods always set my teeth on edge.

Craig shakes his head. "I said no. Too dangerous. Not allowed. Plus, I gotta go."

"So you said," I mumble. "Let's try the other side to get him out of the car.

We slip around the damaged hood to the driver's side door. Craig yanks open the door and grabs for Aaron's jacket collar, as if preparing to force him out.

"Back off, asshole." Aaron smacks away Craig's fist, smearing what is definitely blood onto the knuckles.

Craig gags and grabs hold of the door, hyperventilating and clutching at his chest.

"Don't panic." I rub his back in wide circles while he

remains bent over. "I'll clean it off." Using clumps of snow, I scrub his hand until every trace of blood is gone. "You can look now."

He peeks with his right eye to ensure the skin is pristine before his breathing returns to normal. He stands to full height and looks angry.

"No more trouble from you, mister," Craig commands Aaron. "Get out of the car so I can move it. I gotta get outta here."

"Come on," I say, opting to play good cop to Craig's bad. "You need help. Let's go."

I hold out a hand, which, no surprise, he ignores.

"I'll come in and get cleaned up," he grunts through gritted teeth. To Craig, he sneers, "Then, *I* gotta get outta here."

Craig scoffs and, arms crossed, impatiently waits as we move out of his way.

"Behave," I whisper to Craig before guiding Aaron up the driveway and onto the porch. He sways and nearly falls off the landing, but I grab his arm just in time. He slumps against the door frame. I support him by slinging his right arm over my shoulders. "Let's get you inside. Just a few more steps. You think you can handle it?"

"Yeah," he says weakly, the fight gone out of him.

He's heavier than expected, and it's a struggle to help him onto the couch. He lies down with an "Oomph," and I release the weight of his body with a heavy sigh.

"That could have been worse."

His gruff "harrumph" indicates disagreement.

"We'll have you back home with Rachel and Jeff in no time."

"Huh?" he asks, puzzled. "Home?"

"It's fine." I shouldn't be talking about fine points with someone with a head wound.

Aaron's eyes close, and I stick a finger under his nose to make sure he isn't dead.

"What are you doing?" he asks, eyes still closed.

"Making sure you're not dead." It's essential that he understands the severity of the situation.

"I wish," he says on a frustrated exhale.

How do I respond to that? *Don't dignify it,* I tell myself, and say, "Wait here. I'll be right back."

I gather antiseptic, ointment, and adhesive strips from the bathroom, then get warm water and rags from the kitchen. With supplies spread out on the sofa, I gently wash the dried blood off Aaron's cheeks while he lies on the couch.

My face is inches away from his when he opens his eyes and grabs my wrist.

I freeze, and the wet rag drips watery blood onto his wool coat.

"Did I hurt you?" I ask.

The specks of silver in his eyes twinkle in the firelight, lending him a fierceness that forces the breath to catch in my throat. A five o'clock shadow traces the outline of his full lips and strong jaw. Aftershave, redolent of pine needles and promises, fills the space between us. Sitting this close has me admitting why I avert my gaze whenever he deigns to engage: He's a handsome man and probably chews up and spits out girls like me before breakfast.

What a jerk.

"You can't hurt me." He swallows hard, searching my face, for what I don't know. It seems he has more to say, but silence weighs heavily, one second, then two. After an eternity, he growls, "I can wash my own face. Where is there a mirror?"

"You almost passed out at the door, so you shouldn't get up yet. You have a bad cut," I explain in a gentle voice. It's odd having Aaron in my house. Having him speak in complete sentences and touch me is beyond out of character. It's disconcerting, to say the least. "I think it's better if I do it. Then I'll get you something to eat."

He looks at me queerly. "For what? Being a good boy?" A glimmer of a smile twitches at his mouth. The compelling look, never before seen, leaves me baffled.

"Yes. But only if."

He shrugs and relaxes back against the cushions, releasing my wrist. The tingling that arose with his touch lingers beneath my skin as I return to my mission.

Once his face is clean and dry, I tend the wound. It's not that long, maybe three inches, but it's as deep as it could be. Dry blood, clotted with black hair, makes for slow going. Though I use as little pressure as possible, his jaw clenches, and he grips the sofa cushion when I encounter bone.

"Sorry. This could use some stitches."

The bleeding starts up again, though much slower than after the impact and head banging against the steering wheel. I fold a clean bit of towel and place it over the wound. "Here. Hold this." He reaches up and presses on the towel while I open a sterile package. "We'll try a few butterfly bandages. They should hold the edges together until you can get to an emergency clinic."

He doesn't flinch when I remove the rag and approximate the edges of the wound before taping them together.

"I'm fine," he insists.

I'd argue, but what would be the point? Waiting for a "thank you" for my first aid prowess also seems fruitless, so I clean up the mess in silence.

"What's for dinner?" he asks before I reach the kitchen to

pour out the sullied water and toss the rags in the laundry basket. I'd almost forgotten my offer. Gone is the feeling of attraction, replaced with the reminder that treating others as inferior is what Aaron does. He expects everyone to follow his lead, regardless of the circumstances. To acknowledge how he messed up my evening plans without care would be a sign of the good manners he lacks.

I sigh and play along. The guy needs kindness in his time of need, even if the rear-ender was his fault. "Roast beef au jus, roast potatoes, and green beans."

"And dessert?"

I laugh with little humor. "I'm sorry, was dessert offered?"

"It was implied." He smiles in that brief herky-jerky way that invites tiny tremors of interest to swirl around in my lower belly and alarm bells of distrust to ring in my brain.

The heat in the room rises, and I reach out and turn down the chimney flue.

With dripping sarcasm, I ask, "Anything to drink?"

"A lager, if you got one."

My jaw drops at the audacity of his request.

His amusement turns up a notch until he's laughing. "You should see your face." His pretty blue eyes twinkle in the fire-light. "I'm messing with you. Water will do if it's not any trouble."

My lip quirks. Aaron Hanson is being funny. Who would have thought it was possible?

He tries to push off the couch, exclaiming, "Ahh!" before cradling his head in his hands.

I drop everything onto the closest flat surface and rush to his side.

"Are you okay?"

"Yeah. Just not okay enough for bold moves, like

standing and helping, apparently." Pain and irritation have him grimacing.

I pat his thigh sympathetically. Guilt overrides irritation for judging his attempt to help. He's in pain, and his holiday plans are just as ruined as mine. I could be more gracious.

"You're fine. I don't need any help, but I appreciate the attempt." I fluff up a few couch pillows and help him push back and get comfortable. "Sit tight. I'll be right back."

Before I make it to the kitchen, he stops me.

"Hey, Faith?"

"Yeah?" I turn and make eye contact.

"Thank you." His look is honest and sincere.

"You bet."

Time to rustle up sustenance for my patient.

*a*aron tosses his napkin onto the plate balanced on his lap after demolishing double servings and a slab of Boston cream pie. He's tall and lean, and I can't fathom where he packs it all.

"Do you run?"

He quirks an eyebrow and asks, "Is that your weird way of asking me to leave?"

"No," I say, in a way that makes it sound like having an injured guest was at the top of my Santa list. "You're stuck with me for the night. I'm just curious."

"I run. Six days a week. Between five and ten miles, depending on whatever else I'm doing at the gym."

"That explains it." I take his plate. "Need anything else while I'm up?"

"No thanks."

He reaches forward, snatches the remote from the coffee table, and starts flicking through channels while I clear the dinner plates and cups left over from our meal.

I return with mugs of cocoa and more water.

"What should we watch?" Aaron asks.

"Well, I was planning to binge a bunch of holiday movies, starting with *It's a Wonderful Life*, but this is fine if that's your thing."

He looks at the screen. A reality star with enlarged facial features yaps at another, accusing her of some trumped-up offense with a pointed finger. I can't tell who's who. These shows churn out an endless supply of vapid, low-grade actors. Still, I somehow recognize it. Sordid, popular things seep into the lives of the innocent, infiltrating via the ether, multiplying and staining everything pure and good.

Lightening quick, he hits the guide button to locate the movie, claiming, "That is not my thing. I don't own a TV, so I don't even know what that was."

"Sure," I say with a smirk. "Whatever you say."

He rolls his eyes and hands over the remote. "Can we just watch the movie?"

"In a minute. Are you feeling okay?"

"Yeah-h-h," he draws out the word.

"You went gray again, for a second, like when we were on the porch. You may have a concussion, and I don't want you passing out."

"I'm a bit lightheaded, I guess. What are you gonna do?"

"Check in on you every couple of hours."

"That's passé. You can let someone with a concussion sleep."

"I think that's someone with a fever," I argue.

"No. You're blending adages." He ticks them off on his fingers like he's some holier-than-thou adage expert. "You feed someone with a fever. Starve a cold. You let someone with a concussion sleep."

"I'm pretty sure you mean 'Let a sleeping dog lie.'" Being a pest is one of my strong suits.

He sputters, "No! I mean, don't wake me up when I fall asleep."

Pleased with the result of my hectoring, a giggle escapes my lips.

Whenever Jeff has home classes, I seek opportunities to involve family members, as Jeff's social engagement skills are a key focus. But I'll admit that sometimes it's a bit of payback. Like the time Jeff wanted to raise a caterpillar and watch it become a butterfly. Aaron had bitten my head off for cheering too loudly when Jeff proved he could hop on his left foot ten times without stumbling. Pardon me for encouraging someone's success!

I sent Aaron outside to gather food for the caterpillar while Jeff and I unpacked the specimen that had arrived in the mail. Aaron returned with a handful of inchworms, thinking they were what the caterpillar needed, forgetting that caterpillars eat leaves. I showed him the paperwork to clarify the instructions: we needed to provide the right food for the caterpillar's stage, not something for a bird. Accepting this, Aaron spent an hour searching the neighborhood for milkweed leaves, which Monarch Butterflies prefer. Too bad we had a Black Swallowtail, which feeds on plants from the carrot family, like parsley or dill. So back out to the search he went.

Petty? One could argue. But not exactly when you know both sides. I can't help wanting revenge after being mocked for being a "woo-woo" teacher, as if I'm waving rattles and doing rain dances. Every time I explain the tested theories behind my teaching, he scoffs and rolls his eyes like I'm trying to sell snake oil. Half the time, he ignores me; the other half, he's glued to my side, nitpicking every move. Honestly, it's a mystery how he manages to get his own work done.

Plus, if I'm honest with myself, I find Aaron most

appealing when he's on a mission. There's something about the way he pushes up his sleeves, shows those muscular forearms, and bears down on a task with utter determination. His level of concentration is intoxicatingly masculine, and the intensity engages my feminine sensibilities.

Aaron spends most of his days at home because of work, his sister's, and his. Rachel is a Boston paralegal who works long hours, five days a week. Aaron, a remote graphic designer, helps his single-mother sister. I remember this generosity when his attitude frustrates me. Somewhere in there is a good man, even if he's mastered hiding it.

"You're messing with me." Aaron's features soften at the realization.

A gal could get used to a pleasant Aaron.

"I am." I can't suppress a grin. "I'll let you sleep after we watch the movie."

"Thanks a bunch." A brief yawn, hidden behind his hand, has me wondering if he'll make it that long.

###

The movie ends with me swiping at tears and ensuring Aaron's snores are authentic. He's going to be mad when I wake him, but I'm grateful he's not witnessing my sappiness.

I move to his side of the couch, lean over, and shake his shoulder. "Hey, sleepy head. Wake up."

With a jerk, he sits up, exclaims, "Ahh, shit!" and collapses back, gripping his forehead.

"Are you okay?"

"Killer headache." He squints through the pain. "What time is it?"

I look at the clock on the cable box. "Ten-twenty."

"Morning?"

"It's still nighttime."

He groans. "I told you not to wake me up."

"You don't want to sleep in your coat and clothes. I got my father some pajamas and stuff for Christmas; you can use them instead."

"Got any ibuprofen?"

"Sure." I grab a bottle stashed in the side table drawer and hand it over with a bottle of water.

"Stop!" I yell when he shakes out triple the dose. I slap his hand, and the pills go flying.

He takes a deep breath, in through the nose, then slowly back out. "You are starting to piss me off. Can I take care of myself here?"

With a condescending, "Questionable," I hold out my hand and order him to give me the bottle back.

"And what if I don't?" The bottle gets tucked behind him with a playful wink.

Without thinking, I press my palm to his bandaged head wound, then immediately pull my hand away and hold it over my mouth, stunned by my own impulsive action.

His anger is palpable.

Stuttering, "I'm sorry," I talk fast to cover my awful blunder. "But these can cause bleeding, and we've had enough of that for tonight."

He places the bottle on the coffee table with great care and focus and stands up. "And I've had enough of this," he states, lurching for the front door.

I follow close behind as he swings the door open. The wind slams it against the wall, shaking the room with mighty force. Snow follows the gale, prancing merrily without a care or an invitation to land on the already wet carpet.

"Please don't go. I'm sorry. I reacted without thinking." I'm talking double-time. "You'll never make it home in this.

Walking to the end of the driveway is dangerous. I panicked when I saw all those pills in your hand. It was like—" I stop before saying more than he needs to know.

"Like what?"

He stands with arms on his hips in a wide stance, determined to irritate me into telling the truth while my throat feels congested with memories I'd rather forget. I clear it behind my fist. "Um. Like nothing."

He crosses his arms, dissatisfied with the answer.

"Okay. Like the bleeding you did earlier. You know. Like I said, um, they—the pills—you know, can cause more bleeding." I stand straight with my weight evenly distributed to prevent my feet from shifting further. The behavior makes me look guilty, which I'm not. I'm just unwilling to offer the truth. I prefer to ramble and sound stupid. "So, um, yeah. Like that." I maintain eye contact to indicate that I'm not lying, even if I am.

"Whatever. Keep your secrets. We all have them. But stop playing nursemaid. I'm not your student."

"But, what if—"

He silences me with a finger against my lips. I want to both smack it away and suck it into my mouth to roll it around on my tongue. *What the hell is wrong with me?*

As though reading my mind, his gaze lowers to my lips and leisurely follows the edges, memorizing their shape.

My exhale is a cross between a gasp and a moan.

Aaron's eyes lock onto mine. The allure is powerful enough to replace the physical hold he has on me. He removes the finger that was shushing my lips and rests his hand on my shoulder.

"You don't have to worry about what ifs." His voice is thick and low and terribly sexy. "Life is more fun if we're prepared for all that can be."

Huh? His touch has cost me IQ points, but he's not interested in a response.

He crosses the room and returns to the couch. Removing his coat and scarf, then unhooking his belt, he ignores my gaping. Mesmerized, I stand stock-still, wondering how far he's willing to go. His shirt gets untucked and unbuttoned, and then he tosses it onto the growing pile of clothing. The pants are unzipped and left to hang, low-slung on his hips, dangerously close to falling down.

My eyes follow the tawny skin of his broad shoulders, past the contour of his defined pecs, over his flat stomach, where the firelight adds shadows to a subtle six-pack. The taut flesh tapers into the waist of his boxers. My finger itches to run along the elastic band and peek inside.

He catches my stare and offers, "You're welcome to watch me strip, but now might be the right time to gather up those clothes you offered."

Shaking myself back to sensibility, I rush out of the room and close the bedroom door behind me. I slump against the wood and tap my head against the grain. *Stupid! Stupid! He was getting revenge for you poking his bandage.* A sound not of my making joins the chorus of my self-deprecating thoughts. Childlike fantasy has me wishing it's the jingle of Santa's sleigh bells. But the blushing and embarrassed adult in me recognizes the raucous laughter of a man who sees right through her.

4

A rooster crows, forcing my dreams of warm, sunny beaches away and thrusting me into the frigid morning. I snuggle deeper into the bedding and will myself back to sleep, but it's not happening. Curiosity has the better of me. Is it still nighttime, or has the storm continued to rage through the morning? Taking a cautious peek under the curtains, I discover the storm holds its ground. Mixed precipitation taps a dreadful song against the window pane. No unwanted guests will be leaving this morning.

I'd love to stay wrapped up in bed all day, but I suspect Aaron wouldn't allow it. I wrap myself in a bathrobe and head to the bathroom. After giving myself a once-over in the mirror, I get to work on the overriding impact of sleep: brushing my teeth, pulling my hair back into a messy bun, and pinching some color onto my cheeks. A bit of lip gloss can go a long way, and I swipe some across my lips before declaring myself fit to face the day.

Aaron somehow slept through the bird's announcement. He lies peacefully and still on his back, rolled up in the crazy quilt my mother stitched by hand many years ago, with his coat thrown over him for added warmth. The fire went out overnight. My second order of business will be to spark the flame after checking Aaron for any further signs of life.

I hover over him, watching for the rise and fall of his chest. He scares the crap out of me when his eyes snap open. My heart jolts. I jump back; my knees slam the coffee table, driving me to sit with a loud "thump."

"I survived the night," he croaks, voice thick with sleep.

"Must be my stellar nursing abilities."

He squints, and I wonder how he can disagree. But he surprises me when he mumbles, "Must be."

"How's the head?"

"S'okay." He stretches with a mighty yawn. "It could be worse, considering." He watches me rise, rubbing my backside, on my way to look for any remaining embers in the burnt-out ash. "How's your butt?" he asks, noticing my discomfort.

"None of your concern," I tell him prissily, kneeling to stoke the fire and add kindling. The dry wood catches, and I add larger pieces. Satisfied it will remain burning, I check the flue to ensure it's open and pull on the chimney crane to grab the kettle. A shake indicates that there is plenty of water for coffee, and I center the kettle over the blue-orange heat.

"You know I'm fine, right? It's a scratch. If not for the storm, I'd have left before you woke."

"Your car isn't going to start. You might as well get used to being here for the duration. Craig can give you a lift when he tows your car."

Instead of showing gratitude or indicating he heard me, he asks, "What are you doing?"

"Making coffee." I sit on the opposite end of the couch and pull a corner of the blanket onto my lap.

"No coffee maker?"

"No power."

He flips a nearby light switch up and down and says, "No shit."

It already feels like a long day.

Aaron jerks upright when the cock crows again.

"You have chickens in the house?"

"No. In the garage."

"Should I even ask why?"

"Because they smell too much to let them in the house."

Dissatisfied, he throws me his look of disdain, head tilted, brows scowling, baby blues hard and uninviting. "Tight as it is here, I'm not sure chickens in the garage is a better idea. Maybe if you buy a henhouse? The feed and grain store across town delivers."

Taking a page from his playbook, I ignore the jab.

"The flock is a part of the permaculture garden at Divergent. The principal didn't feel safe leaving them in the coop. And, if you met Angela, you'd know why she wouldn't be part of a solution. She's terrific and intelligent, but those nails, that hair, and her collection of stilettos prevent her from doing anything more hands-on than schmoozing at fundraisers and filling out report cards, which she excels at. I figured, what the heck? I'll bring them home, get some eggs, and my handyman can power wash the cement floor when they leave.

"You hungry?"

He stares at me, silent.

"What?"

"You want me to eat garage eggs and drink coffee brewed in an iron pot over an open fire. Is living in the Stone Age some tradition where you're from?"

"Don't be silly! The chickens needed a place to stay. I had

the room available. Sound familiar?" I give him a dose of his own medicine and shoot him a dirty look.

He makes a show of looking around the room. "Not exactly roomy, but you've made do." Light dawns as he pauses and shifts from sarcasm to teasing. "Ah. You're referencing the Christmas story of the Bible. Gave me a room in your stable. Cute." His smile, suddenly genuine, quells my anger.

Once his words register, I exclaim, "It's Christmas! Merry Christmas, Aaron!"

"Merry Christmas, Faith. I'm frightened. Er, I mean, I'm looking forward to spending the day with you." He spreads his arms wide, taking in the space. "Back in time. At the start of Year 1, apparently."

"You never had it so good," I say, defending my hostessing skills. "You'll see."

ॐ

With legs tucked under me on the couch, I cradle my hot cup of coffee before glancing at Aaron. I lean forward and ask the question gnawing at me, "What possessed you to go for a drive in a blizzard?"

The crackle of the fire and the wind in the distance create a cozy, festive feeling. Aaron holds his mug close, closing his eyes as he breathes in the aroma, and his tense posture begins to relax. We find a rare peace and sip, sighing at the shared comfort between us, the anxious start of the morning forgotten.

"Doing my sister's bidding." He shakes his head. "She insisted it couldn't wait."

"What couldn't wait?"

Aaron reaches into the pile of clothes, finds his coat, pulls a small box from an inside pocket, and hands it to me. "Your Christmas present. When she found the gifts you left, she realized she'd forgotten to put them on the table where you leave notes and updates. She pushed me out the door with strict orders not to return until you had the gift in hand. I didn't plan on a truck being parked on the street as I turned the corner."

"He keeps his lights flashing for safety," I mention.

"Hm." The sound comes through pursed lips. "We'll let the insurance adjusters hash it out."

Wishing to distract him from negative thoughts, I ask, "Can I open it now, or should we wait?"

"Wait for what?"

"I don't know. When do you open presents on Christmas? As a child, my parents let us open one gift before breakfast—a huge spread and a gift in itself—and then open the rest before lunch. We'd toss any clothes into a pile for Mom to figure out later and spend the afternoon playing with our toys and drinking cocoa. One present, generally the most coveted, was saved to open after dinner. It kept the zing alive all day." The recall leaves me grateful and warm. Christmas felt magical as a child. "How about you? What was Christmas morning like in the Hanson house?"

He glances at his watch.

We have nothing but time, so I'm unwilling to let him off the hook. I gaze at him wide-eyed and wait for him to begin.

Rolling his eyes, he caves. "I suppose we were traditional. On Christmas Eve, Dad read *'Twas the Night Before Christmas*. Mom tucked us in early in case Santa started his night of gift-giving at our house. On Christmas morning, Rachel and I were under strict command: no one went downstairs without our parents. Christmas was the only day of the year my mother seemed to tolerate children, so we were never tempted to sneak down before them and ruin the détente. They were early risers, anyway, so we'd be tearing open our gifts before sunrise." As the memories surface, his wistful smile gives way to a frown. "Those days seem like a different lifetime. Everything changed once Mom found her calling." He puts "calling" in air quotes. "Turns out, not being a mother was her life's purpose. She took off with Ned, her nitwit boss, when we were twelve and fourteen. Soon after, Dad remarried a shrew, and, ah—" The sudden silence signals pain, and he leans forward, reaching for the coffee.

"Refill?" he offers, lifting the cast-iron pot.

I hold my mug out for a refill. "You okay?"

"Water under the bridge." Gesturing to the box in my hand, he asks, "You gonna open that?"

Unsure if I should push his dodge, a childlike longing to see what's inside overrides. "I thought you'd never ask." I tear into it, the shreds of paper falling like confetti to the floor.

It's a beautifully carved wooden box. I run my fingers over the swirled grain, admiring nature's handiwork. Nestled inside the green silk lining sits a snow globe, no bigger than a golf ball. Its exquisite craftsmanship suggests it's handmade.

"Where did you find this?"

"I made the box. Rachel, the snow globe. We agreed to incorporate the academy."

The brick building sits in the center, surrounded by a garden in the back, complete with a hen house and fruit trees. A circular driveway and a small parking lot are located out front, similar to the actual grounds. I give it a shake and watch as snowflakes settle on teensy leaves, the roof, and the lone car parked in a space by the main door. It's red, just like mine.

"This is exquisite," I tell him, my tone reverent. "The

detail is incredible. That's my car." I point to the miniature sedan. "And that's a flock of chickens by the apple trees. Oh, my gosh! She painted a classroom scene in the front window, and the teacher's hair is as dark as mine. What did she use for a paintbrush? A spiderweb strand? How did I not know she was an artist?

"And you! The translucent stain brings out the wood's natural beauty. Look how the protective layer of polyurethane gleams in the firelight." The grain tells the story of the tree's age and injuries through the delicate rings and intricate whorls from burls. "You could get lost in the art and symmetry."

I notice that the hinge has an extra piece of metal protruding from the mechanism. "What is this?"

"A lock." He pushes the tiny hook with a fingertip and encourages me to lift the top, but it won't budge.

"A magic box! I love it so much. Thank you!" So moved by the gift, I forget the man beside me is snooty, shut off Aaron, and leap toward him to plant a kiss on his cheek. Things go sideways when he fends me off with a raised forearm, catching me in the solar plexus. Unable to adjust mid-flight, my torso crashes into his face, and the underwire poking out of my most comfortable bra, hidden under my bulky sweatshirt, penetrates the butterfly bandages protecting his wound.

Fresh blood pours down his forehead. He swipes at it with the arm not used for fighting my affections, which is still stuck between us.

I push myself back to my side of the couch, mortified as I try to figure out what just happened.

"You okay?" I ask.

"Yeah." The blood doesn't spray, but it leaks down his cheeks. He dabs it with a napkin.

"I was just happy. Sorry."

He shakes his head with an agreeable smile. "It's okay. I'm not one for physical displays. You surprised me. I hope I didn't bruise your belly...or your pride. It's not you, it's me."

"I bet there's a story there." I squeeze his hand, bracing myself for a blow if friendly gestures fall under "physical displays."

He squeezes back and taunts, "You'll never know."

"Be that way." I shrug a shoulder and sniff. The scent of copper infuses my nostrils. Blood smells terrible.

I need to make amends, again, and ask, "How about I make it up to you?"

"That sounds dangerous."

"Harhar. I bet there's still hot water in the tank for us to take a quick shower."

"Um. Your attempt at gratitude caused enough damage," he says, hands held in a defensive pose. "Showering with you might be the death of me."

I choke on my own spit. I wasn't offering to bathe together! "That's not what I meant. You can go first. That's the olive branch, not...that!"

"Okay, just keep your distance, lady."

He stands up, looking a bit unsteady on his feet. I offer him my arm for support. He hesitates, considering whether to refuse, then sighs and accepts my help, gripping my arm for balance.

"No more Florence Nightingale shit once my head feels better."

"You got it."

5

*B*eing cooped up isn't terrible. But when Aaron acts like Aaron, it isn't so wonderful, either. We try to avoid bickering over my cramped house and Craig's sullenness by playing cards and Monopoly. Frequent food breaks help. We packed the contents of the fridge and freezer into the growing snowbank on the porch to keep perishables safe. Who knows when the power will return? Storing food outdoors in winter is a practical option. It makes me wonder what the point of a refrigerator is when it's freezing. Teachers value any savings. As ever, Aaron thinks my idea is dumb.

"You'll attract animals." He tosses down two cards.

I deal him two and take three.

"How? Most of the food would freeze before the scent carried."

Oooh! My full house is sure to win me the last sugar cookie.

"It's cold. Animals get hungry and come looking," he warns. "I fold."

"No fair! That's the third time in a row you've thrown the game; I want an actual win, not a forfeit. Show your hand."

It's a royal flush, ten through ace, all hearts.

"What the heck? You won."

"Yeah, well." He rubs at his neck, not making eye contact.

"Are you cheating?"

"No!" he says, defensive, but confesses, "I play on a team every Friday night when Jeff goes home for the weekend. I don't make money at it. We're just a bunch of guys who love the game, and we play against similar people for the thrill. Winning here, when you're just having fun and not as serious about it, didn't seem fair since I have so much more practice."

"But it's a game of chance," I argue, annoyed by his sarcasm and frustrated that I lost.

The thickly iced cookie portraying Santa beside his toy bag taunts me. One student's mother is a professional pastry chef, and her tinned treats are a rare honor. Thoughts of the crisp outside and chewy inside, melting on my tongue, have me drooling.

"I'll make a deal with you, I offer. "We'll split the cookie." I hand him the plate so he can do the honors while I pour us more hot chocolate.

"I feel fatter than yesterday," he says, eating his half in a bite and chasing it with cocoa.

"You're eating a lot."

"You keep feeding me."

After the cookie, we lapse into silence. I tell myself I'm content, but Aaron's mention of Jeff tugs at my thoughts. Why does it bother me so much?

I cast a suspicious look. "What do you mean by 'when Jeff goes home?'"

"What?"

It's a simple question. I repeat. "What did you mean by 'when Jeff goes home?'"

"Nothing."

"Yeah. Right."

Divergent Academy remains a small institution where educational rules are strictly enforced. Students are eligible to enroll if they live in Brumal Heights or any of the three surrounding towns we serve. Aaron's expression, as I press the point about his interpretation of the word "home," hints that someone may be bending the rules.

"Let's go for a walk," he says, changing the subject.

"What?"

"We seem to be suffering partial deafness from close quarters. Let's go for a walk!" He yells as payback for speaking to him like a child. "The wind's died down, and I'm feeling closed in."

"Answer my question. What did you mean? Where does Jeff live?"

"I'll tell you on the walk. Promise."

He's definitely lying, but once this guy clams up, nothing moves him. I remind myself I can't let this go. Honesty is non-negotiable in my role. If there's a rule bender here, I need the truth—not just for my job, but for the school's future. One wrong move, and a scandal could ruin everything.

It's still snowing, and the streets haven't been plowed for hours. Taking a walk is low on my list of things to do, but Aaron's persistence in avoiding my questions makes me reconsider. He may be more willing to open up in a less confining setting.

Worrying is second nature to me. Craig's last thumbs-up emoji gives some peace, but my nerves prickle. Living on a quiet street means slow plows, but tonight, it feels like isolation. I remind myself to stay calm, but doubts churn just below the reassurance.

I push back the curtains. Snow and ice tap a dreary Morse

code: It's freezing. Despite the chill, the view outside is breathtaking with everything cloaked in white.

"I have snow shoes," I muse, tapping a finger against my chin. "And my brother left his cross-country skis here, the ones I gave him for Christmas a few years back." I'm hit with a spark of insight before asking, "Do you think he didn't like the gift?"

"I dunno. I'll enjoy them, though. What size shoe does he wear?"

"Eleven."

"My exact size." Aaron offers his hand and helps me stand. "Let's go. I feel stronger and less fuzzy-headed. Let's test it."

Playing outside in a blizzard sounds foolish, but his enthusiasm is contagious.

"Okay. I'll grab outerwear so we don't freeze to death. You get the shoes and skis," I direct, pointing at the side door. "They're hanging over the water heater in the garage." The fresh air could help clear our minds.

A winter wonderland greets us. Snowdrifts climb in some places, while others lie bare, revealing dormant grass—especially under trees. The snow arches in graceful curves, halting to circle trunks with rings of near-bare earth. Snow clings thick on trunks and presses heavily on branches, defying gravity. The path beneath wears a thin layer of ice. We traverse it together but not alike. Aaron's skis swoosh over the snow, while my shoes crunch through the icy layer. He's a gazelle; I'm an elephant.

Instead of focusing on my awkwardness, I absorb the hush of falling, lace-like flakes. The deserted cranberry bog Aaron chose has cathedral quiet, with its stark boundaries between land and water, enhancing the moment's stillness. Softer than an autumn leaf's descent, the faint sound is enough to hold our attention. We lapse into a companionable silence, content in the hush.

Soon, the effort of our exertions catches up, and we're forced to stop and shed a layer or overheat.

"You okay?" we ask simultaneously during a break.

"You're the patient," I remind him. "You go first."

"Moving is what I needed. With the wind at my back, I'm ready to shush home and spend Christmas with Rachel and Jeff," he says, steering us back to his recovery and holiday plans.

His words make me inexplicably sad. Perhaps his orneriness is growing on me, but it's his sexy smile that comes to mind. I realize I don't want him to leave, though I don't want to admit it aloud. Shaking the image clear, I say, "Unwise. That's ten miles from here."

"Sixteen, actually. But you're right, too far. With you in a hospitable mood, I'm enjoying Christmas—for once."

It's hard to know how to respond to being insulted and exalted at once.

Something about his statement needles at me: my odometer registers 10 miles when I drive to 1038 Sycamore Street, the address for which I'm reimbursed for mileage. Our charter's future depends on transparency. If Jeff doesn't live with his uncle, then whose house have I been going to? The stake is whether Jeff is eligible, since the extra six miles could mean he lives just outside the approved range. I can't ignore the possible implications, but pressing further right now might ruin the mood.

"I recommend we keep moving. How about that?"

The wind snatches my hair, whipping it across my face, blinding me. Maybe I've watched too many saccharine movies, but somehow, the air between us crackles. The sharp tang of winter, balsam, and ice surrounds us—my pulse

pounds. Hot, exercise-fueled endorphins charge us with exhil-
arating potential. My breath hitches at Aaron's smoldering
look. Suddenly, nothing tempts me more than the heat of his
mouth on mine.

I shift closer without thinking. He meets me halfway, and
soon our bodies connect from chest to knee. He brushes my
windswept hair back, then cups my chilled cheeks in both
hands. His rough palms radiate warmth, and I can't resist
pressing into them, their heat a shield against the relentless
storm. It's the setup for the perfect holiday interlude until
Aaron goes and ruins it.

He takes my hat, pulls it over my head and ears, and tucks
stray hairs underneath. "You'll catch a cold out here. Let's
move."

Survival leaves me no choice but to follow. My heart has
betrayed my mind. I no longer think of Aaron as a snob, but
he sees me the same way he did before our near kiss. I curse
myself for being easily swayed and focus on putting one
snowshoe in front of the other.

"Wait." He stops me with his arm. "What's that?"

Up ahead, a tiny creature struggles to crest the steep
embankment. A lone Douglas fir tree is all that sits between
the black ball of fur and a narrow but swift stream. The track
that follows his miniature paw prints leads straight to the
bottom of the tree, where the snow surrounds it as if it were
landscaped to expose the ground.

"Oh, my word!" I cry out and push past him. "It's a
puppy!"

I run, awkward in snowshoes. As unabashedly fearless, it
runs towards me, squealing. Ignoring Aaron's rabies warning,
I pursue cuteness and scoop the pup up. About the size of a
large snowball, it fits between my palms.

"Oh, you precious, furry gift! Where is your momma?"

Its tiny pink tongue gets stuck to my wool mitten when he gives it a taste before curling up and getting comfortable.

"How cute are you?" I can't stop kissing the puppy's soft forehead, dripping with melting snow.

Aaron slides up next to me. "Holy crap! He's maybe five weeks old. What's he doing out here?"

"How do you know his age?"

"My family raised show dogs–miniature poodles. Sometimes, we bred them. From what I recall, this peanut has the same abilities and limitations as a five-week-old puppy. He looks healthy, better than I'd expect as a young stray. Mom must be nearby."

The sensible place to look is beneath the tree, where the puppy came from.

"I'll go." Aaron removes his skis and sinks to his knees. He pushes through the snow, using a pole to help maintain his balance. The closer he gets, the louder the growling sound.

"She's here. A mixed breed mutt, under twenty pounds, if I had to guess. She's nursing two other puppies."

The growling increases, interspersed with a few snapping snarls.

"I don't think she'll let me touch her."

"Well, we can't leave them here. Let me try."

I tuck the puppy between my base layer and sweater and ease down the slope. When I stand beside Aaron, Mom leaps up and lunges in a mock attack. Her pups fall off the nipple, scramble to find warmth, and whine over the interruption.

"You're okay, Mom." I hold my hand out so she can sniff my glove and learn we're not a threat.

Mom's not buying it. She bites the fabric on the middle finger and tries to tear it off.

"Yikes!" I yank my hand back, and she lets go.

"Bad idea," he accuses. "Mothers are the most ferocious animals."

"You're the supposed expert." I lash out, still hurt by his failure to indulge in a romantic moment. "What do you suggest?"

We step back from the den and reconsider our options.

"What if you lure her with the puppy you already have? I'll grab the others and use them to make her follow us home."

Darn it! That is a better plan than sticking your hand into a ferocious mother's mouth.

"Let me figure out where to put them before you show her the baby." He pats his coat pockets and then peers inside the one on his left. "These should be big enough for them to fit."

They are tiny.

The puppy in my pocket yawns when I interrupt his sleep. So precious! I can't resist kissing him before holding him lower so Mom can see.

"Start walking backward," he whispers. "Slow and steady."

Unwilling to allow her babies to be stolen, Mom follows me just as Aaron thought she would. She's confident but wary, seeing me as a threat to her and her progeny. She matches my steps as Aaron gathers the remaining pups without getting caught.

Once I'm back on the trail, I walk in circles to keep Mom at bay.

Aaron joins me, and we stand side by side. The dog paces and licks her lips, nervous for her offspring, but she isn't brave enough to attack when we close ranks.

"We'll sweep the area to ensure there aren't any other rogue puppies, but since Mom seemed content with the headcount and there weren't any more trails or prints leading to or from the den, I think we have them all.

"Unfortunately, I need the poles to ski. It would take hours to break a trail back without them. We'll make sure she knows we have everyone, and you can use your lure as a reminder from time to time."

Men are so adept at taking charge. I'm grateful for Aaron's skill, as latent maternal instinct has me in turmoil. I want to give Mom her babies back. It's not right to separate them. I also want to sit on the trail and kiss and cuddle them, breathing in their sweet puppy breath for eternity.

Aaron reminds me I can have both.

"Let's get going. We'll get the pack home, and once everyone is warm and dry, you can snuggle them to your heart's content."

It takes us twice as long to return due to frequent reminder stops for Mom and comfort adjustments for the babies, but we make it safe and intact.

6

*O*nce the fluffballs are tucked in the wood basket, Mom sniffs each head and seems satisfied. She still won't let us touch her, dodging every attempt by tucking her tail and fleeing to the corner. At least she's stopped baring her teeth when we so much as blink. Maybe she's too weary from the journey. Or perhaps she's relieved her babies are warm. Regardless, it seems progress is being made.

"I'll set these guys up in the bathroom," Aaron offers, taking the soft quilt from the back of the couch. "It's the smallest room, and Mom will feel safer there. You rustle up some food–heavy on the meat with veggies, light on the carbs. The babies should still be in the early days of the weaning process unless somebody dumped Mom before she gave birth, so don't include them. Just me and Mom."

Aaron is a genius at the self-serving segue.

I'm pretty hungry, too, after all the exercise and worry. But I'm also freezing as snow thaws through my clothes. This is the coldest I've ever felt. I head to my bedroom, quickly peel off the wet layers, and stand in my bra and underwear. I need warmth before doing anything else.

Unable to resist the fire, I cross the carpet and stand before the glass fireplace doors, rubbing warmth into my arms while the air heats my skin.

Aaron whips around the corner, causing me to jump.

"Whoa!" he exclaims, not averting his gaze.

I try to cover myself, but my hands can't decide where to land. Should I hide my unmentionables or divert attention away from my belly? What about the dimples on my bum, sure to reflect in the glass? I must look like a windmill gone berserk.

He looks at me, his gaze lingering, and I can't tell if it's admiration or confusion.

I'm so bad at flirting and relationships. Society has tangled everything so much that I avoid online dating and setups—maybe unwisely, since I want children and I'm in my prime childbearing years. As a teacher surrounded by other people's children, I sometimes fool myself into thinking my own needs are met. But Aaron's presence reminds me they aren't. Suddenly, my body is screaming: *I want a baby. With him.* My ego can't bear the thought that he might be repulsed by me. I want to sweep all the vulnerabilities under the rug.

"Are you judging me?" I ask, trying to avoid eye contact. Given his textbook-appealing physique, he could be.

My curvier female body is, um, how should I say this without hurting my own feelings? An acquired taste. Taken part by part, it may not make a whole lot of sense. However, if you look at it together, you can solve the riddle. The appeal becomes apparent when you notice how my large breasts accentuate my short but evident waistline. My wide hips make my bum look symmetrical, though one cheek refuses to round as plumply as the other. And, though my petite legs may not be willow branch thin, they have lovely definition.

"I didn't mean to embarrass you."

"Then could you look away, please?"

He shakes his head hard. "I promise. I'm not judging you, but if I were, I'd say Damn! You look good, girl."

My insecurities prompt me to resist the compliment, but there's relief and delight as I sense he means it. *Aaron Hanson likes my body!* I do a happy dance on the inside, a beam of confidence breaking through.

Clearing his throat and averting his gaze, he jerks a thumb towards the living room. "Mom and puppies are snuggled up on the quilt. They'll nap for a while after all they've been through. I'll, um, ahem, stoke the fire while you finish getting dressed."

I release the hold of my belly once he's gone. Breathing never felt so fulfilling.

❧

"Should we worry? They haven't made a sound since I brought them food and water. Do dogs snore? If the snow keeps falling, what will we do? Mom is so drained, and barely had energy to watch with one eye when I peeked. The puppies didn't wake, but they'll need to potty soon."

Aaron talks around his sandwich. "They're fine. They've been through a lot. I imagine they'll sleep for a while yet, maybe overnight."

"Can dogs hold it that long?"

"Depends," he says, pointing to the pickle and potato chips remaining on my plate.

I push it in his direction so he can finish the rest.

"Don't make it a big deal. The floor is lined with newspapers. Puppies go to the bathroom a lot, and Mom is welcome to use them. A blizzard isn't the right time to worry about how housebroken they are."

"I suppose," I sigh, itching to play with my new roommates.

He takes pity on me. "Do you want me to shovel a path off the back porch? We can wake them up to empty their bladders."

I clap my hands and bounce on the sofa cushion. "And play with them!"

"If," he pauses with a harsh look, "and only if they're interested."

"You're all about the rules, aren't you?" I tease, but he stiffens.

A telltale eleven appears between his eyes. "Doing things the right way keeps everyone safe. Life is too unpredictable to go by the seat of the pants. Being an adult means following rules to maintain order. Otherwise, bad things happen." As he speaks, his voice tightens. The shift is subtle: his rigid attitude, at first seeming habitual, now reads as an urgent need to protect himself.

He cringes when my hand reaches out and rubs his shoulder, pulling away slightly at the contact.

"You've been hurt. I'm sorry."

"Haven't we all?" he says, rising so fast the chair almost tips. He gathers our empty plates, blocking my attempt to help. "Do you want to bring the dogs out or not?"

Knowing he's shut down, I let the issue drop and try to ease the tension. "I'll get shovels and meet you at the back door."

On the way out, I press an ear to the bathroom door, listening for signs of life, and hear nothing.

Drat.

Shoveling is more punishing than I expected. It takes ages to get off the deck because we have to hack through the frozen layers. When we reach grass, wind blasts snow over cleared spots as fast as we throw it.

"What a pain! This shit is never going to stop falling," Aaron calls over the screech of the wind. "I'll shovel a short path to a circle a few feet wide. They won't need more space than that." He takes the shovel from my hands. "You're shivering. I can finish up. Go in and get warm."

I'm ready to bolt inside and gather an armload of puppies when Aaron stops me.

"Don't touch them until I get inside." When did he get to know me so well? "We don't want Mom on the defensive with you alone."

Darn his sensibility, but it's a smart call. "Okay. I'll wait for you, but shovel fast!"

Shaking his head, he releases my arm and returns to work.

I feel guilty leaving Aaron with the heavy lifting, but gratitude wins as warm air greets me inside. His chivalry warms me more than the fire. We've connected more in the last day than in the past three months. This new closeness stirs something deeper in me; is it about Aaron, or just the need for connection? He's shown himself to be a true gentleman, and I wonder if my feelings are for him or a more ancient, internal ache.

The more I think, the more it feels like this longing feels bigger than Aaron. Life was different before modern comforts, so is technology to blame? If so, who would give up modern convenience for a deeper connection? Is it too late to simplify?

*a*aron bends over, clutching his stomach, laughing. He's watched me face-plant into a snowbank yet again while chasing puppies. I've never had so much fun!

Mom watches from the sidelines, not missing a move. Her swirly black-and-tan baby clings close, too scared to join the fun.

The two whirling dervishes swarm around us like bees around the queen. The light brown female, with a white swath across her face, uses my fallen state. She climbs up my side, her tiny, sharp nails catching my jacket as she stumbles up. Her brother, all black with white highlights, licks my cold cheeks, his tongue sneaking up my nose. I clutch him and inhale.

"Puppy breath! I'm in heaven."

I smooch his cute face to encourage more kisses.

"Could you be any more strange?" Aaron jeers, offering his hand to help me up.

"No," I admit. "Just one more hit."

The puppy snuffles his cold, wet nose around my face, then bites my nose so hard I tear up.

"Ouch! That's enough," I gasp. I take Aaron's hand, and he pulls me up so fast that the puppies tumble onto the soft snow.

Mom ambles over, nudging the pups by the butt until they do their business. She acts as if we might leave them outside and lies down. The babies settle around her for warmth, snuffling through her fur for sustenance. Aaron distracts her with cheese while I gather the babies. Mom follows us into the mudroom, easily swayed by the bribe.

"Let's dry off by the fire and give them names," I suggest, placing the pups in a basket before kicking off my boots.

"We'll let the mother decide if her babies need a nap after all the silliness." And just like that, the arrogant attitude is back.

"Hey," I protest, shaking out of my coat. "You enjoyed it as much as the rest of us."

"It was okay," he admits with a pained expression.

His sudden mood shift cools me; a subtle prick of irritation rises beneath the warmth from earlier. "Fine. Don't take part. See if we care."

He grabs my arm before I storm off.

"I'm sorry. I'm—" He pauses, looking down and absently stroking the skin around his bandage, clearly struggling to find words. His earlier enjoyment seems to drain away, replaced by fatigue. "I'm tired. At the risk of sounding childish, I need a nap. I can't keep up right now."

I step closer and inspect the wound with my fingertips. "Of course you need to rest. I'm sorry. I should have remembered."

"Not your job." He lets me off the hook.

"I am your acting nurse."

He quirks an eyebrow.

"Not good at my job, I guess," I admit.

He pulls me close, hands on my hips. "I don't know about that. Laughter is the best medicine, and you had me laughing at your athleticism with the pups."

"I was a ballerina for six months in preschool," I brag.

"It shows," he whispers with sarcasm.

"Thanks."

His eyes search my face before landing on my mouth. His attentive look is electric.

A shockwave of desire runs down my spine at the hunger in his gaze. Alone with Aaron, without Jeff and our lessons, I see beneath the surface. Forced together in this tiny space, his annoying habits reveal insecurities. And, darned if Aaron isn't also decent and caring. My dislike was armor, and now, those walls are crumbling.

"What is it?" I press when the silence underscores my own hunger instead of hiding it.

"It's you, Faith. Always has been." He rests his forehead on mine. "Since we met, I've felt a pull as if a cord attaches us. No matter the distance, you're on my mind. I can smell your perfume, hear your laugh, see your face, and I freeze. I've never felt or said this to anyone. How have you thawed my heart in a blizzard? I want to kiss you, but I'm afraid I'll never stop—not today, not ever."

He's just given voice to everything I feel, but I'm skeptical of his change of heart. My heart pounds, exposed. Fear and promise spiral through me as I struggle to find an elegant response.

"Please." If the word sounds unsophisticated or like begging, so be it. I need him like water in a heat wave.

His lips touch mine, feather-light, exploring with both the sweet tentativeness of a first kiss and the heat of an expert. Our breaths mingle as the kiss deepens. He plunders my mouth with perfect balance—tongue and heat, inhale and exhale. Our mouths perform the sultriest duet, leaving us fulfilled but still oh so unsatisfied.

Aaron tears himself away, stepping back from my embrace, gasping for breath, eyes to the ceiling. "We can't," he insists.

I disagree and reach for the hem of his sweater. My fingers sweep across the solid warmth of his abdomen.

He groans and stops my hands. "Don't. You're killing me. I want you, but I can't give more, not now. You don't know the effect you have on me. Going further is foolish, and I'm no daredevil. I'm holding back to keep us from getting hurt."

His words stun me. I shake my head. "I thought you hated me, found me beneath you. You called me 'Jeff's glorified playmate' when your neighbor stopped by, and now you're waxing poetic."

Aaron shakes his head and wraps his fingers through mine. "I don't hate you. Never did. I was wary of you. You made my throat close up." His chuckle is soft at the memory. "I actually thought I was allergic to your perfume, but it's something far worse." His Adam's apple jumps under the skin as he nervously swallows. "Against my better judgement. I've developed deep feelings for you, Faith Quinn. A feeling I've never felt before. I wouldn't wish it on anyone."

O holy heck! How do I respond? *"Take me, I'm yours,"* sounds right, but I hold back. He needs time to figure things out, and I'm still catching up.

Aaron rakes his hands through his hair, wincing as the bandage tugs. Shakily, he says, "This is too much for both of us. Maybe I should go, clear my head on the skis. After the school break, we'll know if this is real or cabin fever. I'm at a disadvantage with all these details rattling around in my mind."

"Maybe it's your head wound?" I venture, even though my feelings flummox me, too.

I make him laugh, giving us a much-needed break from the intensity of our conversation.

"You're tired. Nap now, and we'll talk after the break or when you wake up." I wrap my arms around his waist. He hesitates before returning the hug.

"I'm glad you got that off your chest. I'm confused, too." I meet his gaze. "I thought I had you pegged: Aaron the Arrogant."

"That's what you called me?"

"That's right. And I'm not taking it back. You still tend towards bossiness and know-it-all-ness, so it is an aspect of your personality."

"Hey—"

I cut in. "Can I finish?"

He clenches his jaw but allows me to continue.

"I also see that you're caring, albeit guarded, and smart, but willing to share what you know." I share a saucy grin. "Plus, you're a hell of a kisser."

"Why, thank you." He bows at the waist theatrically like an actor on Broadway at curtain call.

"How about you lay one on me and then lie down for an hour or so? See how you feel."

"I can tell you how I feel already. Warm, connected, and horny as hell."

It's my turn to laugh. Seeing this side of him makes me want to discover more.

"Then kiss me, horndog," I demand, and he does so deliciously.

8

While Aaron naps, I study the canines. The nervous Mom stays distant except when tempted with treats. She prefers beef over chicken and apples over bananas. The pups devour everything as if survival depends on it—and I suppose it does. I've observed their personalities enough to jot down possible names. Aaron deserves a say, so I curb my excitement about favorites.

Mom's coat is like aged wood: amber and black swirls, a dull patina. With nourishment, she'll likely shine. The runt of the litter looks just like her, so choose Swirl, Fauna, Violet, Ice, and Brilliance for them. And in a nod to Aaron's crafted Christmas gift, I add Treasure and Jewel. The other puppies differ. Fawn, Amber, Apricot, and Varnish are best for the brown female. For the snuggly black male with white feet: Onyx, Socks, Licorice, or Bon Bon.

I picture Aaron—focused, evaluating, never unsure as he rejects every name. That unshakable certainty can be reassuring, but sometimes it feels as restrictive as a straitjacket. Am I too sentimental, picking endearing names for survivors? Should their names match the harshness of their reality? I cling to the idea that a bit of softness could heal wounds I can't see. One can never discount me overthinking a problem. Perhaps he'll surprise me and like all the names I've chosen.

All this thinking, combined with the fire's warmth, makes me want a nap. I sink into the couch cushions, snuggling the pups. The storm rages outside, but, in contrast to the coziness inside, it brings drowsiness rather than a chill.

I must drift off, because when I open my eyes, the fire burns low, the puppies huddle at my belly, and Mom curls into the V behind me. Note to self: drop the temperature and become more appealing.

I don't want to move, but my feet are numb, and my bladder reminds me that the puppies will soon need to go out. We've only had them for a day, but already we're as synchronized as sorority sisters on their periods.

I chuckle at my observation and wonder if Aaron would find it amusing. On second thought, he believes I'm weird already, so I'll keep it to myself.

Before I can work out how to remove the puppies from my lap without waking them, Aaron approaches and gently places his hand on my head, smoothing my hair.

"Hey." His deep wake-up voice rumbles my favorite way. "How long was I asleep?"

I tilt my face up to his. "Couple of hours."

His rhythmic strokes move to my cheek.

"We'd better get them outside."

"I got it," I offer as I rise. "Keep an eye on them while I use the bathroom." It's becoming an emergency. "And I'll start water for coffee."

I push the chimney crane over the fire, squeezing my thighs close together, and add another log on my way to the bathroom.

Aaron lurks outside the door when I'm done. "Nature calls," he quips.

After pulling on my coat and snow pants, I can't resist taking a picture of the puppies in the wicker basket. It takes a moment for them to settle down, but the shot turns out perfectly. Gold and Myrrh flank Frank, with all three chins centered on their paws, clutching the edge.

The photo gives me the perfect excuse to check in with Craig and find out about the storm and his safety. I hit send. He responds immediately, saying he's been working through the midnight hours, driving deserted Brumal Heights streets, waiting for someone to care.

The governor extended the state of emergency. I'll be plowing your street in a few hours. Could you leave something to eat in the mailbox?

True to form, he finished everything I packed up earlier.

I respond, *Of course.*

Thanks. Cute pups, BTW.

I send a heart emoji, notice my battery is at 30%, and decide to leave a note with the food. I then suggest we communicate as if we were from the 1900s until the storm passes. Craig is our only connection to the outside world. I don't want to lose contact.

Against nursing advice, Aaron joins me outside to help with the dogs. The puppies play around while their mother tries to get them to focus. It isn't happening. They're too energized from their nap and scamper around, chasing snowflakes and digging up buried sticks.

"How much power is in your phone?" I ask.

"Dead as a doornail," he admits. "Why? You thinking of ordering a pizza?"

"Hilarious. No, I'm nervous. Craig said the state of emergency was extended. The weather app claims we'll see snow for another 24 hours. Yesterday's forecast promised it would stop by now."

Aaron wraps me in his arms, pulling me close. The solidness of his chest feels safe and warm compared to the blizzard's chill.

"We'll be fine. We have food and water." He gestures with one hand to the puppies. "Great entertainment. Being stuck inside is claustrophobic after a while, but we can go exploring whenever you wish. How can I help make the situation more tolerable?"

My body aches from the last outing as darkness falls. After relaxing in warm sweats by the fire, I'm not particularly motivated. I lose track of time. Have we been trapped for days or hours? Aaron remains positive. I teeter between a desperate need for escape and the wish that time would stand still. Isolation feels like suffocation and freedom, in equal measure.

"Tell me more about yourself, Aaron. Learning what makes people tick fascinates me and is much of why I helped start an alternative school."

He leans back, surprise written on his face. "You were there from the beginning?"

"Mm."

"You barely look old enough to be a teacher, let alone a maverick."

I cringe at his assertion. "I didn't start Divergent Academy alone—there were three of us: me, Angela, and Grace. We met in our freshman year and have been friends ever since. No 'three's a crowd' stuff." I still marvel at how special these women are. Few meet such open-hearted, intelligent people. "When they met my brother Zane, they treated him like everyone else. My family wasn't used to that. Most people avoided us. I think their fear was really about his lack of bodily control.

"Let me back up. Zane was delivered early at eight months. Not quite a premie, but oxygen deprivation made him act like one. Progress was slow. He came home from the hospital at four months, still acting much like a newborn.

"My parents hired all sorts of caregivers. Zane progressed in his own way. He couldn't hold his head up, but he made eye contact when it was held steady. By age three, he cooed and made guttural sounds. His smile, rare but genuine, showed he was present and worth every effort." I pause, recalling his sweet face—faded to black and white over time, adding to its appeal. "He loved anything soft: teddy bears, velvet, stress balls. Loud noises, bright lights, and sand upset him.

"People fear what they don't understand and would give us a wide berth in public. Zane was intellectually limited. We always hoped strangers' reactions didn't hurt him. For him, it was normal—not knowing anything different until meeting Angela and Grace."

Our conversation breaks off when Mom-pup suddenly barks and charges the fence.

A tiny pink nose pops through a gap in the pickets and sniffs the air.

"Look out!" Aaron yells and runs into the hissing, snarling fray.

I'm unsure who he's warning, the dog or the cat. Neither seems inclined to back down.

Aaron quickly reaches over the fence, grabbing the cat by the scruff with one hand while supporting its furry bottom with the other. The cat yowls and struggles, but Aaron holds steady and tucks it under his arm in a secure football hold.

"Room for one more?"

"Gee. I don't know. My home was accused of not being 'roomy.'" I point at the guilty party, who looks chagrined.

"Don't be petty. A homeless cat will fit into any size space. You'll see."

"What do you think?" I ask the orange-and-white tabby cat, scratching its head. It doesn't lash out at me, but keeps an unwavering focus on the dogs. "What about the dogs? Aren't they enemies?"

"You worry too much. Let's get everyone inside."

Before we do, we get the babies to settle down and finish their duties like good puppies. Then, I lure them and the mother with a trail of treats until they're all locked in the bathroom.

Aaron carries Tabby into the mudroom. We haven't reviewed dog names, and my battery is low, so Tabby will have to stand as the cat's name for now. With the dogs settled in the bathroom, I lead Aaron, with the cat, toward my bedroom—the only other room with a door. As soon as he sets Tabby down, it ducks under the bed.

A million questions spin around my brain. "What are we going to feed a cat? What do we do about litter? Can you teach a cat? Is it feral? Will it attack me when I'm sleeping? Aren't cats nocturnal? Will it let me sleep? Wanna switch rooms?"

Aaron grabs me by the shoulders, giving them a shake before mimicking slapping me across the face, hitting both cheeks. "You need to calm down," he says.

A sudden flare of anger jolts through me at his mock-slap, even as I know he's only teasing. The heat in my chest surprises me—I hadn't realized how tense I'd become; apparently, some lines are still too raw to cross right now.

"Be careful when telling a woman to calm down," I warn, fists clenched. I recognize that melting down won't help, but the more I urge myself to relax, the tighter my muscles get. I wonder why I'm coming undone when just this morning I welcomed the rapid changes. Now, Noah's Ark feels less comforting. Maybe being trapped with Aaron, which I find both alluring and infuriating, is what's setting me off.

"Faith, honey." He places a hand against my cheek. "I'm teasing. Everything will be okay. I'm here. I've had lots of experience with animals. You don't have to do anything you don't want to. Let me make dinner. You sit and have a warm drink by the fire."

"Oh, no!" I race from the room and into the kitchen with Aaron on my heels, yelling, "What now?"

"I promised to leave more food in the mailbox for Craig! He's out there busting his butt so the rest of us can sit on our asses. He'll be crushed if I forget, not to mention starving."

Aaron studies me as I open cabinets and fill a brown bag with snack packages of raisins, nuts, and crackers.

"You're an independent thinker."

I stop and scoff at the comment. "Do ya think? I'm thirty-two and never married. I've been on my own since college, and I avoid adult relationships like the plague because the human species is so damn damaged. It's why I work with children. As messy as their learning disabilities can be, at least the world hasn't broken them yet."

The concerned look on Aaron's face worries me. I look over my shoulder, expecting to find Craig wondering why I failed him or, at minimum, the mother dog tilting her head, wondering why we're holding them hostage, but there's no one there. His sympathy is for me, and something inside me breaks.

I double over, wrecked by a surge of emotion I can't contain. One minute, I'm handling life like a boss, and the next, tears stream down my face, burning with frustration and shame. The abruptness shakes me: I had felt strong, but now I'm undone—sobbing in my kitchen, blindsided by longing and exhaustion, with a man I want to seduce and strangle in equal measure.

Aaron comes close enough to touch, but he keeps his hands to himself as I keen and wail. He hands me tissues and offers me a glass of water before he stands silently nearby to allow my release.

Sitting at the kitchen table, the crying was an unexpected release, making me lighter and looser, tinged with a hint of embarrassment. *Why can't I be alone when I'm having a breakdown?*

"You okay?" he asks when the silence thickens.

"Yes. No. I don't know." My voice shakes, clogged with tears and exhaustion. "Maybe I'm storm-crazed."

He pats my knee and hands me more tissues. "I think you could use some rest. You're used to managing things alone, and you've been gracious, but I suspect having a visitor, one you don't know that well, wasn't on your list for Santa. You've shifted from confident host to overwhelmed caretaker very quickly. But I'm here, and I'm not going anywhere."

"I bet you want to." My head rests on my folded arms on the kitchen table, shielded from his gaze and the weariness that comes with letting go.

"No, I don't. Despite everything, this is the best Christmas I've had in decades, and it's because you're here. Most days, I'm numb, moving through life on autopilot. But you—you set something alight in me. You're remarkable, and I don't know what scares me more: wanting to know you or realizing you make me want to know myself. That feeling terrifies me, the vulnerability unfamiliar."

"You don't like any of it?" I ask, thinking about the burning kisses we've shared.

He catches my drift and backpedals. "Some of it is worth keeping, but all these sappy feelings and thoughts, puke."

"I'm right with you," I admit. "Falling is scary."

"I suppose it's this way for everyone stuck in similar circumstances. Guy hits the truck and obtains a head wound. Gal gives up a peaceful holiday to taunt him with her saucy ways."

I laugh at the condensed version.

"There it is, that beautiful smile. We're going to be fine. Just let me take care of you, at least for tonight. See how you feel about it. Could be addictive." He raises his eyebrows and tilts his head with his signature grin, sexy and amusing. "I'll even finish packing the feed bag and put it in the mailbox. All you need to do is sit on the couch, kick off your shoes, and let me take the wheel. Can you do it?"

It sounds delightful, but it's clear we're both skeptical. "I'll try my best."

"I suspect you always do," he says, squeezing my arm. Then, with a kiss on my forehead, he begins running my home.

9

"No," Aaron rejects all the potential dog names with absolute authority as he hands the list back.

"Why not?" I scan the curated names.

"They're stupid."

"They're not! 'Brilliance' means smart. 'Licorice' fits—he's yummy." The pup yawns and licks my palm.

Aaron leans over and strokes the pup. "Good boy! Always praise them when they aren't using their teeth on your hands. All puppies go through a teething phase, but for now, we'll lay the groundwork for behaviors we want to see for a lifetime."

If I knew about dogs, I'd call him out for mansplaining. My jaw tightens at his stubbornness; every word feels like a challenge I can't win.

"You think you can do better?" I nod at the names.

"Mom's their north star. We found them at Christmas. Her name's Bethlehem—Beth for short. Dogs like short names."

"I'm not stupid," I snap back.

"Never said you were."

My mood sours. "Can we move on? I'm sick of calling them nouns and pronouns."

"That's not very teacherly," he mocks.

"I'm not a public school teacher. We're accredited but not government funded, so we do as we wish." I shrug. "Within reason."

He folds his arms, one brow quirked, lips pressed tightly.

"Seriously! We march to our own drum. We pledge allegiance and pray every morning."

"What?" He gasps, clutching his chest. "Prayer. Oh, the humanity."

"Yeah, yeah. Prayer shouldn't have been removed from schools. Believing in something greater helps humble us; we've forgotten that in our thirst for autonomy.

"The prayers are inclusive, if that helps feed your skepticism. Students take turns leading; creed doesn't matter. We even ask kids from atheist or agnostic backgrounds to share a poem or suggest a moment of silence. The mountain is the same; the paths differ."

"Is that saying on your letterhead?"

I give him the hairy eyeball, daring him to back down.

He grins, cool and unbothered.

"No. But a student stenciled, 'Our weakest moments teach us the most powerful lessons,' on the lobby wall. The art department's top artists painted a mural around the quote depicting a crying child on the playground, surrounded by other children offering help. A brilliant sun, dragonflies, and hearts add whimsy, balancing life's challenges."

He hums, nodding smugly. "Just what I expected. The classic PC manifesto."

In the interest of peace, I offer a new topic. "What are the dog names you think are so superior?"

"Thought you'd never ask." He winks, picking up the pup

who resembles Mom. "The girls are Gold and Myrrh, the boy Frankincense."

He's good. I googled all my ideas, and he didn't use the internet for help once

"Gold and Myrrh work, but Frankincense is too long and, as you say, stupid."

He sighs. "We'll call him Frank. So there you have it, four respectable names."

"Who says I agree?" I want to wipe the sanctimonious look off his face, even though I like them.

"Don't be jealous. I've done this before."

He gathers the puppies and sings them a nonsensical song, using the new names in the chorus. The tune is reminiscent of "It Came Upon a Midnight Clear," though he takes considerable artistic license. No surprise, with all his other talents, his pitch is a spot-on, resonant baritone.

You came upon us at noontime, Dogs,
*   a scruffy bunch of four.*
*   You stalled our outing on Christmas morn,*
*   We stopped to lend a hand.*

Now we've named you the furry quad,
*   Beth, Gold, Myrrh, and Frank to celebrate our day.*
*   This, this is the be-est day,*

I bet even Faith would agree.
*   If she could only re-e-ecognise*
*   How amazing Aaron can be.*

.   .   .

My irritation melts away as he serenades the puppies; a warmth builds where annoyance was. Yet, I still feel a pang. I'm jealous of how his affection flows to them so easily when I crave it for myself. A reluctant smile tugs at my lips, realizing maybe Aaron's oversight comes from my lack of floppy ears and black bean toes.

Ego slips away, allowing me to admit, "The names are perfect. This day has been perfect—"

He cuts me off with, "I think you're perfect."

"Naw." I wave my hand and move closer, blushing at the compliment. "You'd think differently if you could read my mind."

Aaron pulls me closer with his arm around my shoulder.

Beth must feel left out. She leaves the fire, presses against my leg, and sighs when I scratch her ears. Her trust display feels like a genuine compliment.

"You think I don't know how I come off?" Aaron asks.

"If you did, wouldn't you change your tone?" His deep, metronomic voice rumbles through me as I lean my head against his shoulder, making me no longer care about the answer.

"Not now," he says.

"Why? What makes now so special?"

"I have your undivided attention. I can't think of anything I wouldn't do to keep it."

"How can you switch from the most recalcitrant person I've ever met to the man who says everything right in the blink of an eye?"

"Innate talent."

"How about we practice something you're even better at?" I involuntarily lick my lips in anticipation.

His affirmative answer is the sultriest kiss he's laid on me so far. Until he bests it with the next and the next. My toes curl with pleasure as I sink my fingers into his thick hair. Aaron leans further into me until I'm pressed beneath him.

He lifts his head and gazes into my eyes, supporting his weight on his forearms. "Let's never leave here," he says.

"My home or this moment?" I ask.

"Both," he answers before slanting his lips over mine and continuing the kissing me senseless portion of the day. Since the sun has set, we practice long into the night.

ॐ

Later, as we lie together, I kiss the arrow-shaped birthmark curving around itself, as it points in a southerly direction down Aaron's neck.

He stirs awake. Wiping a hand over his face, he asks, "What time is it?"

"Late," I answer.

Distracted by an odd sound, I ask, "Did you hear that?"

"Hear what?"

"Humming."

Aaron cocks an ear and rises on an elbow. "I don't–"

The musical sound starts up again; this time, we make out words. "Jingle bells, jingle bells, jingle all the way," and so on.

Aaron slumps back down on the cushion, groaning as he covers his face with one arm, the other tugging me close. The sound of his heartbeat thumping in my ear has a better rhythm than the chorus outside.

"They won't go away. Carolers want money or food or, I don't know, Christmas cheer, whatever that is."

"I wouldn't know. A midnight serenade hasn't shown up at my door before. Should we get dressed in something less

casual than our pajamas and ask them what they want?"
Leaving Aaron's warm embrace is the last thing I want to do.

"I'm not getting up," Aaron proclaims. "They're being rude. No one invited them to our first Christmas."

As the carolers continue outside and the two of us remain on the couch, Aaron's eyes meet mine, and I sense an unspoken connection. My heart lifts, and the loud world recedes. Our quiet companionship appears to mean as much to him as it does to me. Doubt gives way to contentment.

"I'm not getting up either." I snuggle closer and trace his birthmark with a fingertip. "If I didn't know better, I'd think this was a tattoo."

"God is the ultimate artist," Aaron says. "Every sunrise is proof."

"Deep. Would you consider yourself religious?"

He rolls over so we face each other, holding hands under the pillows, legs intertwined.

"Define religious?"

"Having a belief and practicing it."

"Then I'm religious. God is all around me. I'm always in His chapel."

"Simple. I like it."

We ignore the songs getting louder.

"Hard to discount something so basic. It keeps atheists modest and believers humble."

"But you believe it?"

"And practice."

"You're more complicated than I gave you credit for," I admit.

"Did you prefer me superficial?"

I'm quick to respond. "No! I like this version of you. More approachable. Dare I believe, a bit less arrogant?"

"Your beliefs are your own," he jokes. "But, really. Are you religious?"

"I'm a practicing Catholic: Sunday Mass, confession, all of it. The formula they follow speaks to me. Everything is laid out for you. It's a place I don't have to think."

"Don't all the lies and whitewash around the clergy and altar boys bother you?"

"Yowza! Just go there, why don't you? I can't speak to that without getting nauseated, so let's just say, anyone involved in the crimes or the cover-up deserves an eternity with Satan. I'm there to strengthen my relationship with Jesus and worship Him, nothing more."

"I respect that," He says, kissing my knuckles before pivoting. "Are they ever going to shut up?"

The carolers are becoming hard to ignore. Someone brought a tambourine for caroling. It's not helping the out-of-tune choir.

"I'll get rid of them." I kick off the covers, force myself up, and slip on my bathrobe.

Aaron jumps off the couch. "I won't let you go alone."

He grabs a half-finished bag of chocolate truffles and holds it up. "Does this count as Christmas cheer?"

"It better be because it's all they're getting."

Opening the door, we find the six members of the Yench family, tiered on the steps of the porch. Three women and two men I've never seen flank them from the ground. Belting the song out with zeal, they finish "Away in a Manger," sounding like the cattle the song references.

We clap without enthusiasm when they finish with expectant smiles.

"Tough night for caroling, isn't it, Jessica?" I ask my pert neighbor.

From what I gather, Jessica is a sweet lady and a harried

mom. We don't know each other well. If we run into each other, she's in a rush, carpooling her tykes to sports and sundry commitments. We end each conversation with "Let's have coffee soon," but it never happens.

"Sure is," she admits, with a forced inflection. "But the kids deserve a Merry Christmas."

Her husband, Steve, puts an arm around her shoulder. "We've been cooped up inside, opening what seems like hundreds of gifts. Time got away from us, and the kids were high on sugar cookies, so we decided, what the heck? Let's put them back in their Christmas pageant costumes and take this band to the street. The Crosbys and Alans couldn't resist joining us." He tilts his head back and catches a snowflake on his tongue. "You in?"

No doubt, we're all going a little stir-crazy from being stuck indoors.

Aaron fields the question with a hard "no."

For once, I'm charmed by his brevity. Still, I don't want the neighbors to dislike me, so I make an effort to be polite.

"Sorry." I hold up my hands. "It's late, and we're in our pajamas. We hate missing out."

"No, we don't," Aaron says under his breath.

I elbow him in the side.

"We can wait while you change," Steve offers with a gummy smile.

The others cheer in agreement.

"Oh, well. Um, what I mean is, we were sleeping." I hitch my thumb over my shoulder.

"The rooster rises early," Aaron says, yawning so wide that his uvula, the punching bag in the back of his throat, shows.

No one knows how to respond to Aaron's comment; awkward silence ensues.

Steve wears a puzzled expression as if he's scheming a workaround for our dilemma. Afraid he might discover something to sway us, I use the old standby and wish them a "Merry Christmas," then grab the half-bag of chocolates from Aaron. Thrusting it into Jessica's hand, I retreat backward into the house, fake joy plastered on my cheeks.

Aaron closes the door as the choir makes a slow exit, belting out a painful rendition of "So Long, Farewell" from *The Sound of Music.* My ears will never forget the horror.

"That was a close call," Aaron says with a scowl. "What were you thinking answering the door?"

We shiver at the thought of what could have been.

"I wasn't," I admit. I wrap my fingers around his neck, pulling his head down for a kiss. "Don't be mad. It's Christmas."

Aaron glances at his watch. "Nope. It's Boxing Day, which we Americans don't celebrate."

"We could," I offer suggestively.

"What does that mean?" he asks, seemingly unwilling to let go of my transgression of opening the door to revelers.

"Come on. Let's go back to bed, and I'll show you."

I take his hand with a sultry look, and he follows without further question.

10

*A*s hard as it is to admit, Aaron makes it easy to rely on someone. He tuckered out the pups, fed the chickens, and even lured the stray cat from under the bed for some attention. Turns out, Pounce is a neutered male who loves chin scratches and hates belly rubs.

Aaron enters the living room after tending the animals. He sets down the next meal and says, "Hope you're hungry." The plate features a fried egg and cheese sandwich on wheat toast, accompanied by baby carrots. He carefully pours a mug of hot coffee using his mastered pour-over technique, then places it beside the plate.

"Wow. Thank you." I can't remember the last time someone prepared a meal for me. This alone could make me dependent on someone.

Aaron mumbles, "You're welcome," around a bite of his sandwich, and vibrant yellow yolk oozes down his chin.

I reach over and wipe it off with a napkin.

He swats my hand away, grabs the napkin, and finishes the job.

"So." Aaron looks guarded. "You never finished telling me about your brother. What happened to him?"

I'd forgotten our earlier conversation, maybe on purpose. Years have passed since I last spoke of Zane. As the memory returns, tears sting my eyes. What if his birth story resembled mine? Am I ready to trust Aaron, someone I didn't consider a friend until today, with my most painful story?

Because Aaron has proved steady, I brace myself and start. "Remember when I smacked the pills from your hands?"

He snorts.

I hit my forehead, remembering my idiotic move. "I know! But I had no control over my reaction."

Staring at my meal, trying not to shake, I confess: "I found Zane." The memory surfaces, harsh and bright, like a silent movie I don't want to watch. My hands curl tight around my fork as I force myself to keep talking. "It was a week before college. I'd never been away from home. Fear and excitement twisted in my gut as I imagined the next four years. In short, I was self-absorbed.

"I'm not so arrogant as to believe that neglecting Zane for a short time made him take his own life. He had closed off and withdrawn from us months before I got wrapped up in myself. I believed my parents when they said it wasn't my fault."

As I falter and my voice wavers, Aaron notices and reaches for my hand, steady and reassuring. He gently clasps my fingers, grounding me as I'm about to get swept away into yesterday. The warmth of his hand signals safety and reassures me that I can remain present.

"It wasn't my fault," I repeat to make the words stick. "But finding Zane, so still in bed, his skin already cool, was my undoing. He seemed to be biding his time. He was on so many medications. We decanted them into organizers to keep them straight. We kept the box over his bed, out of reach. Someone left it by his bedside. Somehow, he swallowed enough to stop his heart.

"The doctors said it was a peaceful death, and if his expression were any indicator, I'd say they were right. I never saw him look so content. Like he'd just figured out the secrets of the universe."

"Maybe he did," Aaron says. "I'm sorry you lost him. It seems as though he was done living a life dependent on others and chose to make his boldest decision count."

"That's a healthy way of looking at it." My stomach rumbles, breaking the heavy moment and reminding me I'm famished.

"Eat before you get hangry."

After I nibble at my sandwich in silence, a recollection interrupts my focus. "How rude of me. I had asked you to tell me about your family before cutting in with my story. You go this time."

"Seems anticlimactic."

"This isn't competition. Everyone's story is unique and fascinating. I want to know yours."

"You sure?"

"Please."

"Okay-y-y." He looks like he's sucking on a lemon. "Where to begin? Umm."

"This should be good." I tease.

"Good? I don't think so. I've come to see that having children was my mother's biggest regret. Even on her happier days, we felt like a waste of time. Need a ride to baseball? She was busy. Stuck on science homework? Her degree was in liberal arts. 'No cereal? Here's a dollar. See if the cafeteria has something to tide you over until lunch.'

My father was even less available. Rachel and I raised ourselves. I escaped into art, which led to a career in graphic design after quitting jobs that didn't pay enough. Too bad Rachel didn't have an escape. She lost herself in Vinny, the jerk who helped her make Jeff, before vanishing.

"I love my nephew, but being left in the lurch with a disabled child wasn't something I wished for my sweet sister." He tries to smile and make light of things. "We had nice Christmases, though. It was the one day of the year my mother didn't punish us."

"I'm sorry you had a rotten experience. That's not fair. This may not help, but imperfect parenting is common. I see it often in my work. Our lottery admissions bring in students from diverse backgrounds. Many parents miss the mark.

"Were you able to salvage a relationship with your parents as you got older?

"No." His violent head shake says it all. "We would get letters when they moved, but nothing indicated they had changed. They left behind angry landlords and unpaid bills, always acting as if they were entitled, as if the world owed them a free ride. If the best things in life weren't going to fall into their laps, they'd just steal them.

"When Jeff was one, and the doctors noticed delays, Rachel asked for help. She needed practical assistance. Jeff was colicky and barely out of infancy." His laugh is cynical. "My mother agreed to fly out and assist, but she just started fights and caused drama.

"One day, Rachel called me panicked. The baby had been screaming for hours. My mother locked herself in the spare bedroom and refused to leave. We didn't know her husband had left her for the neighbor, and she had nowhere to go. Mom didn't come to help—she came because she's a leech.

"When I got to Rachel's after her hysterical call, my mother had her against the wall, slapping her, while Jeff screamed in her arms. The years disappeared, and I was ten again, forcing my mother off my sister. The scene and emotion were indescribably awful." Aaron's faraway look shows he's lost in old pain.

Life's challenges don't leave anyone alone.

I place a hand on Aaron's arm. "You okay?" I use his own strategy, pulling him back to the present by asking simple questions.

"Are you going to eat some more?"

The sandwich has been held in midair since he began talking. He looks at the food with a startled expression, shrugs, and gobbles it down.

I hand him the coffee. "Drink?"

He drains it through clenched teeth.

"Feel better?"

The hurt shows in his eyes, but he continues. "The cops came and forced my mother to leave. I quit college. I moved back to town before starting a graphic design certificate program. Now we recycle every letter from our parents without opening them. Our father may not have been present for the histrionics, but he enjoyed feeding the fire with gossip. He pitted everyone against each other. So breaking off ties with him was necessary, too."

"Sometimes, the best you can do is let go."

I hold his hands in mine and squeeze. "I wish I could erase all that for you. No child deserves pain like that. The silver lining is how close you and Rachel are. She must be so grateful to have such a heroic brother."

Aaron makes so much more sense to me. How do you not grow up with a distaste for strangers when those who were supposed to love you weren't safe?

"You aren't spooked by my past? Me being the kid even a parent couldn't love?"

My lip trembles as tears pool. The thought of any child growing up starved for love guts me.

Seeing my compassionate expression, Aaron chokes, "Don't pity me!"

"Okay! I just feel bad for you."

"That's called pity."

He presses his hands to his head as his eyes squeeze shut. "I hate going back there. Quick—tell me something–anything to wash those memories away."

I tread carefully, recognizing the hold family has on us. Loyalty can surpass reason. "The longer I know you, the more I like you. I'm sure your parents loved you as well as they could. And if they didn't, shame on them. They were fools. Is it okay to feel that?"

"Hm. I suppose," he admits with a twinkle in his eye. "Got anything else?"

I lean in and press my lips to his.

"I like that even better," he murmurs, encouraging me more by placing his hand on the back of my head and deepening the kiss.

Yup. More is so much better.

Until it's worse, and all hell breaks loose. The roof explodes over our heads, and the dogs scatter like buckshot.

*B*eth bounds up in front of us, positioning herself protectively between us and the timbers crashing through the roof. She snarls, baring her teeth; her hackles spike in a mohawk down her back. Bracing herself in a fierce stance, she locks her gaze on the falling debris. The peace we had vanishes amid disaster.

Aaron and I twist in terror toward the front room, watching as the roof crumbles beneath a massive oak. Wind and snow blast inside, snuffing out the fire. The outside invades, shattering our familiar haven.

As our paralysis subsides, more trees slam to the ground. We leap to our feet. I scream, clutching my chest in shock, while Aaron throws up his hands, palms out, and exclaims, "What the hell?"

The cat yowls from behind the bedroom door. I picture him with hackles raised and nails extended, ready for battle.

Aaron yells over the din of the storm, "Do you have a chainsaw, a tarp, and a length of rope?"

The Hope Diamond could be stashed in the attic's crawlspace. I wouldn't know. My thoughts are buried under the roar and the dread hammering my bones.

"I don't know," I yell.

"Don't freak out." Aaron takes charge, words cutting through the savage decibels. "I'll look in the garage. You get the dogs locked in the bathroom. We'll meet back here and get this squared away."

Leaves, branches, and snow pile at the entry as wind whirls debris into every crevice, devastating my peaceful home. Uncertain, I glance at Aaron for confirmation that we're not going to die before acting. I drop to my knees and reach under the coffee table to coax a trembling Frank from his hiding spot.

"Hey, buddy," I say in a low, soothing voice. "You're okay."

I reach my hand out and let Frank sniff it before grabbing him by the scruff, just as Aaron taught me. Holding him close, I wipe away his frightened whimper with a kiss. Then, weaving around the worst of the branches, I cross the room to Beth.

She relaxes long enough to sniff her baby boy. Once she's sure he's not hurt, she follows me to the bathroom. I scatter a few treats on the floor and shut the door behind me to search for the missing pups. I push through the debris as things calm down.

Gold chose the spot under the kitchen table as the safest spot, while Myrrh skittered behind the TV stand.

Hoisting one puppy under each arm, I carry them into the bathroom. Since bathtubs are said to be the safest place to hunker down during a storm, I line the tub with soft blankets and settle the babies inside. Mom leaps in and curls up. The puppies tumble about until they settle and begin to nurse. The way she calms them with her body is nothing short of a miracle.

I offer a short prayer of gratitude to my family, who treated me the same way. When I had a need, they tried to help me navigate it. Even with all Zane's limitations, my parents did their best to show up for Freddie and me, never minimizing our more typical childhood turmoils.

After talking to God, I notice my shoulders are no longer hunched in tension. The burden eases, and the day feels more manageable. Such is the power of a prayer pause.

Stepping away from the bathroom, I stroll through the dumpster fire that is now my home. Memories resurface, each one tinged with a new appreciation that calms my earlier panic. The difference between then and now leads me to reflect on my luck. Gratitude, no matter the challenges we face, can get us through the worst.

Back in the living room, Aaron appears with a chainsaw gripped in one hand, a rake in the other, and a blue tarp wedged under his arm. A rope coil slung across his chest, Indiana Jones style.

Man, is he sexy!

I walk into his open arms, even though he holds them that way to display his haul. I wrap my arms around his torso and, with my head resting against his chest, I learn a new definition of home.

"You okay?" he asks, kissing the top of my head.

He drops the chainsaw and tarp on the floor and pulls me close.

"I'm good," I tell him, looking up.

"And the doggos?"

"They're fine."

As he holds me, the stress and fear from moments ago

fade into a warm, consuming attraction. Nothing we've said should have my girly parts heating up. Yet here we are.

I rise up on tiptoes and press my lips against his. He tastes like frost, his tongue like mint. His smile widens, and my lips follow suit. As the kiss deepens, someone moans. How yummy! The heat of his mouth fires up my insides and sends my thoughts racing.

I press against him and balance myself with my arms around his neck.

"Puppies," he says, breaking the kiss.

Panting, I ask, "Huh?" His touch, taste, and smell leave me muddled in the headiest way.

"You taste like puppy breath."

Embarrassed, my hand crawls up between us to cover my mouth. "You don't like that."

He grins, the mischief in his eyes making my heart flutter. Slowly, his hands move up my sides, pausing at my bra. With a gentle touch, he unclasps it, freeing me. His gaze lingers, full of affection and desire.

His voice is thick with longing. "I dreamed of you last night," he admits.

I'm struck dumb with yearning, but my hands know how to show what I want: him.

I unfasten his pants and help him with his sweatshirt. Focused on undressing him, I barely notice he's disrobing me, as well, until we're both naked.

Oh, the glory of the fit male form, flesh as art.

It seems I'm not alone in my assessment. Curious canine eyes peek from around the kitchen corner.

It appears that someone forgot to close the bathroom door.

I tuck behind Aaron, shielding myself from the dogs, but

the mood is broken. I can't be part of warping their innocent minds. What must they think, seeing us bare, fur-less, looking as though we're attacking each other?

I forgot how comfortable Aaron was with nudity. He hasn't slowed his ministrations one bit, dropping down to his knees. He twists my body forward and trails his lips down my back as his hands become acquainted with my bum. The luscious sensation contrasts with the curiosity in the pups' obsidian orbs, powerful enough to bore through granite.

"Stop! I can't do this." I slip from his embrace, scurry to the couch, and cover myself with a pillow.

"What?" he asks before Frank stumbles over in his adorable drunken sailor gait and inserts himself between us.

Aaron picks up the fluff ball and nestles him close. "He doesn't mind. Do you, pal? It's the bro code."

Frank bites his nose hard enough to bring tears to his eyes as pinpricks of blood rise from the puncture wounds.

"Ow! Why does he keep doing that?" Aaron returns the savage pup to the floor.

"So much for the code," I quip.

Finding the gauze pads we used on his old wound, I tear one open and soak it with water to clean this new bite. They say a dog's tongue is cleaner than a human's, but who knows? I've seen where they put them...

Nursing my patient has become second nature, and I kiss the tip of his nose when it's clean and dry.

"Better?"

"My nose, maybe." He sighs, hands on his hips, deflated in more ways than one. "I guess the mood has been broken. Can you hand me my pants?" He points to the floor where they landed by my feet.

Before I have a chance to toss the pants his way, Myrrh

lunges forward, grabs the end in her mouth, and pulls while growling playfully. Gold and Frank eagerly join her, and now we're stuck chasing the dogs around the room—still naked—trying to retrieve our clothes.

"All right," I yell after the foolishness shows no sign of letting up. "Enough!"

The puppies stop what they're doing and watch me, fabric hanging from their jaws.

Laughing at their adorable expressions, I approach with a treat held out and trade up. I'm not above a bribe to get what I want. Like offering candy to a baby, they give in without a care.

Once we have them contained again, we dress. The place falls quiet for a blissful moment before reality intrudes. The silence highlights the damage that needs repair, and relief quickly fades as the situation's magnitude returns.

"Where do we begin?" I ask at a loss.

"I'll need a kiss for luck before we do anything."

I give him three kisses, leaving us breathless. I'd love to stay this way and ignore the world around me, but the snow pile continues to rise, turning my living room into a ski slope. It's actually snowing indoors. The wind whips flakes to the ceiling, before they fall on everything. Buckets of leaves join in. How can there be so many leaves in winter? I raked until my hands blistered in the fall.

"I'll tackle the trees. You clean up behind me."

"Got it, boss."

With a solute, I grab the rake as Aaron picks up the chainsaw, and we get to work.

He yanks the starter until the chainsaw roars to life and assaults the smashed oak trunk and tangled branches. Wood chips fly, compounding the debris as the chainsaw's whine duels with the storm. The amount of detritus is so over-whelming that it hurts to look at it.

I start sweeping where I stand. Any progress in the right direction will be a help; something is better than nothing. At least, I hope so.

12

*H*ours later, we collapse on the couch, skin tacky with sweat and smelling sharply of pine sap and acorns. Scraps of bark and brittle leaves cling to our clothes and nestle in our tangled hair.

"How many trees did that oak take down? Are any left, or are they all in my living room?"

Shaking his head, Aaron admits, "Too many. My arms turned to rubber from the chainsaw and hauling branches."

"Sorry, this holiday's been such a mess. Let me help." I muster some strength and slide over to knead his sore muscles. "I'm so grateful you came to my rescue."

He moans at my ministrations and leans into the massage. "So were the chickens," he says.

I suck in a breath–the chickens! I picture the garage and them clucking away, oblivious to the sky falling, and my stomach flips. They could have been crushed had the trees fallen just a few feet differently.

"Are they okay?"

"Not a scratch. Surprising, considering the damage. Even the coop was left intact. I moved it to a safer corner, and they were pecking and clucking as usual when I left them."

"How will I ever repay you for all you've done?"

Aaron waggles his eyebrows. "Sweetheart, I don't have your kind of stamina."

I yawn. "That's not what I meant. I'm wiped. And honestly, you kinda stink."

Aaron lifts my arms and sniffs. "Whew! You're not so fresh either."

"You guessed my surprise. How does a bath sound?"

When he lets go, my arm flops onto the couch, numb and useless, with all the liveliness of a dead fish.

"The hot water tank ran out yesterday."

"Ye of little faith." I push up from the couch and stagger to the fireplace. My body protests with every step, but when I arrive, my spirits lift. The multiple pots near the fire are bubbling with hot water.

"Voila!" I swing back the crane for the big reveal.

He peers over my shoulder with a guttural sigh. "Is it too soon in our relationship to say 'I love you?'"

The words sound good, but I deflect. "Plenty of clean water for us to bathe," I say, before adding "separately," so he can't accuse me of propositioning him again.

"Should we flip a coin to pick who goes first?"

Aaron presses a hand to his chest, mock-insulted. "After my He-Man work, you're doubting my manners? Ladies always go first." His brow rises, and he grins. "And in my world, ladies always come first."

Any other time, with a man like Aaron, I'd jump at the chance to test his bluff, but instead, I laugh in his face.

"You have a problem with that, too?"

"No," I gasp. "I'm punch-drunk, I'm so tired." I can't hold it in and surrender to madness.

Minutes tick by as I keep laughing, Aaron watching me shift from hilarity to exhaustion. When my laughter finally fades, he hands me a tissue and asks, "Feel better?"

I pause, tissue pressed to my cheeks, my laughter echoing in the quiet. Tension melts from my chest, replaced by a buoyant relief. "Yeah. Sometimes a belly laugh is the best medicine."

Tiny pieces of tissue stick to the sap on my cheeks as I look down, waving slightly with my movements.

"Can we just flip the quarter? Giving me first dibs is like you folding in poker. Odds are I have to win sometime."

"Don't blame me for being a gentleman if you lose."

Aaron digs a hand into his pocket, produces a quarter, and flips it into the air. He catches it, slaps it onto the back of his other hand, and reveals the winner.

"I win," I say, with as much energy as I can muster, which is admittedly low.

The uncomfortable ickiness on my skin keeps me from falling asleep where I stand. I'd love to close my eyes, but I'm afraid of waking up with my face on the floor.

"I'll watch the dogs so you can bathe alone. Grab your pajamas—I'll bring in the water. How's that sound?"

"Sounds like all my wishes are coming true." I touch his cheek, relishing the rough texture of his unshaven face. "I can't thank you enough. As bad as everything is going, it's nice to have your company, not to mention help."

"I gotta admit, I never knew teachers led such vibrant and dynamic lives. I thought they were all about grading papers and staring over eyeglasses and yelling sensible things like, 'No running in the halls.' Who knew they fought storms, harbored strangers, and offered kisses hot enough to burn?"

"There's plenty more where that came from," I brag, with zero energy to back up my words.

"I'm looking forward to it after we get some sleep," he promises with a brush of his lips on mine.

I could stay forever encircled in his warmth.

"What day is today?" I ask. Time has lost meaning. The sky remains as dark as when the storm rolled in. Pristine white snowflakes break up the monotonous gray-on-gray palette outside the windows. Has a day or a week passed since Christmas? Has the new year come and gone as we battled the elements, rescued animals, and grown closer?

"Still Boxing Day. The longest day of the year."

So it would seem.

We can no longer ignore our stench. Aaron steps back, arms extended, holding onto me as I head toward the bathroom, until our fingers finally let go.

"Don't lift those water buckets," Aaron admonishes.

"I won't," I promise.

Giving me a thumbs up, Aaron goes toward the bathroom. I collect washcloths, soap, and towels from the hallway closet for our baths and follow him, my arms full.

❦

The baths and a light meal leave us feeling tired, yet too revitalized to sleep. We sit splayed on the couch, nursing beers and talking in low voices; the moment feels sacred and eternal. The blend of well-used muscles and the pull of slumber creates a drug-like quality, making us want to stay awake and ride the vibe.

Puppies nap around us, adding to the somnolent atmosphere, while Beth snuggles on Aaron's lap, soaking up the long, rhythmic strokes against her side. It's a wonder she and Pounce don't get along. They share an affinity for Aaron's touch, just as I do.

Frank raises his head and looks around. Not liking what he sees, he rises and eases onto my lap before yawning, curling up, and falling back asleep. Not to be outdone by their brother, the girls soon wake and scramble, one to my lap and the other to Aaron's. After some shuffling, they settle back down. With their adorable faces and gentle demeanors, these pups should have no problem finding forever-homes.

Mom clearly prefers Aaron—she trusts his touch, his way with her babies, and the calm he brings her. She overreacts to many things, but Aaron's presence soothes her in ways I can't replicate.

"Would you want to keep Beth?" I ask, crossing my fingers.

"Hm," he replies, noncommittal.

"She prefers you, and rehoming might be hard," I say, knowing nothing about dog adoption.

Aaron turns the tables. "How about you? Are you ready for the adult milestone of pet ownership?"

"What do you mean by 'pet'? Don't you mean dog?"

His brows raised. "Have you forgotten the cat in your bedroom? I caught him rifling through your underwear drawer the last time I checked on him. He looks rather infatuated and obsessed."

"Right. The cat." I pinch my nose and squeeze my eyes shut. "Maybe it has a home. We can make flyers when the power's back."

"Maybe."

"But you doubt it."

Aaron shrugs. "Simple statistics. Stray cats are more common than a pack of stray dogs, so."

Cripes! Chickens in the garage, a cat rummaging through my dresser drawers, and a pack of puppies tearing through the house. The overwhelm is real. It's a lot for someone who has never even owned a hamster.

"I'm better with people," I argue.

"Are you?" Aaron wonders.

"Present company excluded, apparently."

"I'm playing with you. No doubt, I'm your biggest fan." As he speaks, he removes the pups from our laps and relocates them to the pile of blankets we fashioned into a cozy bed.

I watch him, curious and a little puzzled about his endgame here. "What are you doing?"

"This," he says, settling in beside me and pulling me close. Eyes closed, foreheads touching, he whispers, "I like us together. If keeping Beth means keeping this feeling with you, then I want that."

"What if the price is you keeping all the puppies and the cat?"

He opens his eyes the tiniest amount, peering at me through thick lashes, unsure if I'm joking, before volleying a counteroffer. "I'd need something in return. Something good."

I plan to kiss his cheek, my intent innocent. But just as I lean in, heat sparks in my chest, fierce and urgent. Before I know it, my lips find his, the ache in my muscles fading into the background as I let the kiss last, breath held, surrendering.

Aaron's surprise mirrors my own; our fatigue vanishes, replaced by a jolt of connection. He grips my waist tight, kissing me deeply, and heat rushes through my veins. Desire sparks, burning away the last trace of exhaustion. When we break for breath, our eyes lock: wide and hungry. Another kiss draws us past uncertainty, and longing pulls us under.

"Faith," Aaron blurts out my name like a curse, gasping for air and pushing away. "I can't—"

I grip him tighter, unwilling to let him go. My insecurities struggle for validation after repeated rejections, and I lock my fingers together behind his neck.

"I like you too much," he says.

"Don't blame me. I'm good to go." To prove it, I kiss him again and place his hand on my breast. Moaning, he gives it a squeeze and pushes one knee between my legs.

Suddenly, he stops his pleasant maneuvers to engage in conversation again.

"Faith."

"What?" I ask through gritted teeth. I don't care what he has to say. I only care about how my body feels: thirsty and dying to be quenched by Aaron's touch.

"What if you regret this?" He sounds so sexy, breathing as if he'll never catch a breath. Having this sort of power over another person's body is the headiest aphrodisiac. "You have to admit, if it weren't for the storm, there is no way we'd be touching each other like this."

"True," I placate him. "But there *was* a storm, and you have my fire raging."

I push up onto hands and knees and shove his shirt up and over his head and shoulders. Aaron flinches like he's being burned when my lips find the exposed skin of his abdomen, trailing kisses downward.

He watches spellbound as my curious fingers find the waistband of his pants to tease out the fun hiding beyond the fabric. He whooshes out a guttural moan, jerks onto his side, and I find myself lying prone beneath him. He holds me down with a hand on my belly, the other strokes the outline of my jaw. The contrast of firm and gentle has me squirming, wanting his hands to continue exploring. I can feel his inner conflict, which heightens my pleasure.

"I want you so much." His look is severe; the words hold

so much promise. "But I'm worried we're reacting to a desperate situation. Promise me you won't regret this."

I don't understand him, so I shake my head and talk tough. "What's to regret? I like you. You like me. We can have this and more."

"I don't take leaps of faith for just anyone," he confesses. "This has to mean something to you because you mean so much to me."

Tears spring to my eyes. His vulnerability startles and touches me, revealing a gentle, sincere side of Aaron I prefer. My longing changes from physical to something deeper and more certain. Of course, I want him.

"I want you. Only you. Now, when the storm abates, and when we return to real life. I promise you that."

He dips his head for a pause before looking at me once again. "Why didn't you say so?" he jokes.

"Because I was busy doing this." My hands roam—words now blend into action. The tension from before shifts into pleasure as we explore each other's favorite spots. Our lists, it turns out, are legion.

13

*I*n my dream, I'm trapped in an interrogation room, hunched at a scarred plastic table with a bowl of rotting leaves. A harsh lightbulb blazes overhead. Alone and trembling, I rub my arms; my fingers are melting icicles, dripping water onto my lap. A chicken crouches nearby, greedily slurping the mess and telling me, "Move, and you're dead."

I still, squeezing my eyes closed and silently screaming, "Cock a Doodle Doo!"

The door slams against the wall, splintering and cracking, huge pieces hanging from the hinges. A pack of small dogs enters, snarling as they rush to my side of the room.

The chicken barks in rage, but it's futile. One dog grabs its foot, another its wing, and the third clamps on the chicken's head. Amid the frenzy, the crack of bones is deafening.

"Cock a Doodle Doo!" I yell aloud this time, pulling on the chicken's tail feathers in that powerless way of dreams to free her from her fate.

Somehow, my efforts pay off. The dogs drop the chicken. Blood drips from their smiling jaws as the bird bolts for the exit and disappears. They turn their aggression, leaping as a single entity onto the table and proceeding to attack me about the head and shoulders. I fight as hard as a person can with defrosting icicle hands and hear, "Ow! Faith, quit it!"

How do they know my name? Are they my captors? Is this a different realm? Have I been abducted by a canine alien species? Have I gone mad?

The answers don't come, so I continue fighting.

One of the dogs holds my arms down, and I fear I'm sunk. Using a tried-and-true, last-ditch effort, I jerk one knee up and hit a different dog on its flank. It howls in a high pitch and demands, "Cut the shit!" while its pack mate continues attacking me.

The fight drains from me. I have one weapon left, and I use it to sink my teeth into the last standing dog's nose.

Except it's not a dog. The entire scene shatters as I wake, still half-caught in dream logic, my teeth clamped to Aaron's nose.

"Are you finished?" He asks, drolly, as I release my teeth.

The details of the stress dream hit me. "Was I talking in my sleep?"

"You did more than talk." Using his phone as a mirror, he moves his head left and right as he inspects his nose. "Is my nose too big?"

"No. Why?"

"It keeps getting attacked, and I'm starting to get a complex."

"You're rather handsome. I'd describe you as having a Roman emperor's countenance."

"Veni, vidi, vici," he quotes Julius Caesar. "I came, I saw, I conquered." Pretty much describes what he's done to my heart during our hibernation.

Returning to the dream, I ask, "How awful was it?"

"You kept yelling 'Cock a Doodle Doo!' and making barking sounds. You were thrashing and biting the air surrounding the puppies until they ran away and hid. I thought Beth was going to fight you when you picked up Frank and tried to knee him in the gut."

My hands fly to my face, horrified by what I did.

Aaron squeezes my hand. "It's okay. You were asleep and unaware. I got between you beasts by throwing myself on top of you. Beth scampered away to check on the others once she understood I wouldn't let her intervene. I'd love to know what the hell you were dreaming about."

As I recount the dream, the boundaries between sleeping and waking disappear. Slowly, the mist fades, and the room's details sharpen as my frontal lobe resumes control over the subconscious.

Awake and alert, I recognize how the dream developed using cues from the real world. First, the rooster crowed, then Myrrh knocked over water during a rambunctious game with her littermates. When the lights came on, the surprise loosened the hold of the dream. It's a relief to be back.

"It all makes perfect sense: my icicle fingers, the 'attack' dogs, and striking out. The shock of having electricity back presented as sinister in my dream," I explain. What a relief to discover that I've retained my sanity. "I'm blaming REM sleep."

"I'm not so sure everything makes sense. Why did you bite my nose?"

"You were holding my arms down. How else could I fight you?"

"You weren't fighting last night when I held you down." He nuzzles the crook of my neck, nibbling at the sensitive skin. "If memory serves, you were squirming in a rather sexy way."

I try to act nonchalant, like he's not making me want to squirm again, with the merest touch and taste of my skin. But it's no use fighting the fact that the slightest attention from Aaron has me willing to do just about anything to get even more.

"So, you like how I squirm?" My inquiry includes a suggestive gyration as I adjust my hips and center myself between his thighs.

Without warning, he stops playing with my neck and rises onto his forearms to gaze at me.

"You don't have any regrets about last night, do you?"

"No regrets except the struggle to wake up like a normal human," I reply. "If I hadn't been processing the stress of the storm and all the oddities that arose from the dream, we could have wrapped our arms around each other and reenacted last night."

He rolls off of me and lies on his side, facing me. "You paint a pretty picture."

I lean in for a kiss, and he meets me halfway.

Abruptly, Aaron sits up and stretches before shocking me mute. "We'd better round up the dogs and work on building their trust back before I leave."

His last word catches me. "Leave?"

"Of course. The lights are on, and I don't want to overstay my welcome."

I protest. "Seems awfully abrupt."

"Endings can be that way. You've been nothing but gracious. It's just time."

I can't believe it. He's pulled the rug out from under me without a care. The warmth of the moment vanishes, replaced by cold certainty: he never cared. I convinced myself he was honest about a new version of "us," but his rapid change of heart is the truth. Nothing new. I was played by Aaron the Arrogant once again.

I'm ashamed of myself when I ask, "What's your hurry?" trying to buy more time to come up with a reason.

"I'm worried about Rachel and Jeff. If the electricity is working, then the streets must be clear. I bet Craig will finish plowing and be back before long."

He stands up and starts getting dressed, talking about how things will unfold as though the words aren't breaking my heart.

"You know your buddy will show up for more food before he calls it a day." He hops on one foot, pulling his pants up the opposite leg as he dictates how it is. "I'll take the dogs out. You start breakfast."

Sitting on the corner of the bed beside me, oblivious to my mute state, he pulls on his socks and continues delegating. "I'll join you in the kitchen once the pups are set. How about making omelets, bacon, toast, whatever is left on the porch? We worked up an appetite last night, and the day is young."

He hasn't noticed that I haven't moved a muscle since he mentioned leaving.

"I'm in for a rude awakening when I get back home without a plow buddy like Craig." He runs a hand through his hair. "I'm tired just thinking about all the cleanup.

"Well," he claps his hands together. "There's nothing for it. Let's get back to our lives."

As Aaron whistles for the dogs, moving through the cold, I watch—stunned, breath caught, heart clenching, unable to move. I ask myself, *What did you expect? Forever?*

His leaving shouldn't surprise me. Logic and our history suggest that his about-face makes sense, but my chest tightens, and tears sting my eyes. I shut down, refusing to beg as the door clicks shut behind him.

⚜

Just as Aaron predicted, minutes after breakfast is ready, Craig returns. The hum of daily routine, powered by electricity, contrasts with the bittersweet atmosphere. Cooking feels simple again. The bitter taste of hot, fresh coffee reminds me of how fleeting life experiences are. One day, you don't like someone, and the next, you're in love with them. Then they wake up and leave you without a care–after eating a healthy breakfast, of course.

Talk about being used.

I look from one man to the next. They shovel in the food, barely pausing between bites to ask, "Please pass the butter." In a pathetic display of revenge, I stick my tongue out at Aaron.

The food tastes better than usual, but it sits like a rock in my stomach. A finality looms, a quiet echo of our moments since Christmas Eve. These were the most dynamic days of my life. Someday, I'll look back with tenderness. For now, nothing changes. Aaron will go home. Craig will stop by to help with projects as always. I'll return to school and routine, my changes invisible, like my bruised heart.

Craig shovels in the food and finishes his meal like it's an Olympic sport. "You ready?" he asks Aaron as he stands up and clears empty dishes to the sink.

Aaron looks up, perplexed. "For what?" He wasn't paying attention.

"You want a ride home, doncha? Credit card or cash for the tow, and tell me which collision center you want it dropped off at." Craig snaps his fingers. "Let's go, let's go."

Even though he brought it up, the surprised look on Aaron's face indicates he's not crazy about going so soon.

I'm ashamed to admit to a glimmer of hope at the thought of him staying.

"I thought you weren't allowed to give people rides?"

Craig shakes his head. "Only during storms. The storm is over, and you have five minutes to meet me outside. If you're late, I'm leaving you and your vehicle behind."

"Craig!" I admonish. "Be nice."

"I am being nice," he argues. "But I've been awake for days. I'll fall asleep soon if we don't get crackin'." He squeezes my shoulder on the way out the door.

Aaron and I sit without speaking, neither knowing where to begin our goodbyes. Finally, he clears his throat. "Faith."

My name on his lips is laced with regret and pain. Neither of us knows what to say. Tension invades the space, and my wish for more gives way to acceptance. I collapse within, as my heart retreats for protection, as the truth settles in: first impressions are always right. *What a jerk!*

"It's okay, Aaron. You have lots to do, for you and for Rachel." I'm strong enough to conjure a facsimile of a smile. "Tell her I said hello and I'll be back for Jeff's tutoring after the new year."

"Ah, uh-okay," he stutters. "Can I do anything before saying goodbye to the pack? Help with the dishes or something?"

The dogs will miss him.

"I'm good." I turn away, grief welling thick in my throat. I force myself to appear calm, salvaging the last of my dignity. I swallow back tears and offer to walk him out.

"No need. Thanks for everything."

He pulls me in for a brief, brotherly squeeze before disappearing down the hall—a quiet, final departure from more than just this place. His absence echoes within the chambers of my broken heart. I stand alone, emptiness closing around me.

14

"Uh-oh. She's got that look in her eyes," Angela laughs. She and Grace link hands and block my path, arms against my chest.

Organizing storm cleanup keeps me busy. After days spent rushing, calling in favors, and barking orders, I fall asleep the moment my head hits the pillow. For now, work shields me from thoughts about Aaron. Time heals as the clock sprints forward.

Grace nods. "Yep. Same flinty look you had when we started Divergence Academy. I thought you'd stab the contractor with those scissors, the way you attacked that ribbon."

Looking over her glasses, Grace tells me, "You have tendencies."

My shoulders slump with a sigh. "One time, ladies. One time, I stabbed someone by accident! When are you ever going to let me live it down?"

The day we passed papers on the property stood out as a community highlight. The local news stations interviewed us and later showcased our venture on the six and eleven o'clock news. Our state representative, always looking for an angle, gained some positive press, offsetting controversy over a new tax increase. Before the official ribbon-cutting ceremony, the entire staff was asked to stand for a photo. My hands shook with nervous excitement. I couldn't wait to begin! Years of hard work—and the pain of losing Zane, who planted the seed, so to speak—were finally paying off.

As we lined up, with me clutching the scissors, Grace supporting the shovel embedded in the dirt for the first scoop, and Angela striking a pose, Jorge Hendrickson arrived and headed our way. The Jorge Hendrickson. Lead actor in such rom-coms as *A Prince for a Paralegal* and *Falling for a Farmer*.

I never expected him to attend the event after receiving my letter. I asked for a signed picture, knowing his story of overcoming dyslexia with the help of a third-grade teacher. At the after-party, he offered his support for our fundraising and promised to help as long as needed. True to his word, Jorge has since brought in major donors, keeping D.A. in the black.

I was star-struck, jaw hanging open. I used the scissors to get Grace's attention. The tip barely got stuck. The skin on her bicep was pierced and was just slightly bleeding. Now, I never hear the end of it.

"We don't have time for a trip down memory lane," I say, trying to push through. They press back. "Come on. Let me pass."

"Not until you eat lunch," Grace says sternly.

I grab a sheaf of rolled-up papers from the back pocket of my jeans and shake them in their faces.

"Have you seen this list? Santa's Naughty and Nice list pales in comparison to what we've compiled for the work crew to tackle. School resumes in a few days. You're holding up progress!" I shriek, nerves raw.

Angela purses her lips, assessing me as if her doctorate were in medicine instead of education. "Hunger-induced hysteria. She needs sugar, fat, and salt. Stat!"

Angela wraps one arm around my shoulders, and Grace follows from behind, forcing me into the kitchen.

"Eat first, run around later," Grace orders, giving me a gentle shove to sit.

In the kitchen, Elaine, the school's social worker, has been cooking nonstop. With practiced ease, she channels the same passion into both her culinary efforts and helping students open up at school. A warm chocolate chip cookie and a glass of milk can work wonders.

As I unfurl the napkin onto my lap, Elaine sets a plate before me: a thick cheeseburger and fries flecked with sea salt. They're a tasty reminder of how long it's been since my last meal.

My rapturous "yum" is resounding and all the thanks Elaine needs. She pats me on the head and tells me to leave room for dessert before returning to the stove to dish up more food for hungry workers.

Angela and Grace sit together, closing ranks on the remaining chairs across from me.

"I don't need supervision," I mutter, mouth full.

Grace holds out her hand. "Give me the list."

With food in my stomach, my brain feels less combative, and I turn over the documents.

Angela marks the pages with a Sharpie pen wherever Grace points.

"What are you doing?" I'm mollified but still responsible for managing the cleanup. My house serves as the central hub for receiving orders and sustenance, so it makes sense that I'm in charge. And everyone knows the list is sacrosanct.

"A lot of these are done," Angela points out. "Let's check them off for a dopamine hit." She hands me the marker. "Go on. Put a line through 'cut firewood' and 'replace the window.' The Martins' and Fredricks' houses are as good as new."

I scan the updated list and am impressed with the progress.

"Wow. We've accomplished so much in just a few hours."

"Many hands," Grace says gently. "Trust us. We've got you."

"Absolutely," Elaine says, setting down coffee and mugs.

Grace pours for each of us, knowing our preferences for milk and sugar by heart.

"Now that we've bought you some time." Grace's tone shifts to business. "Tell us about the hunk you entertained during the storm."

I choke on my burger. "How—"

Elaine clears my plate and lays out three pieces of chocolate cake with vanilla ice cream in front of us like a Blackjack dealer in Las Vegas. We pause, savor, and swallow before they fill me in.

"I was helping at your neighbor's house. The Yench's deck lost a few boards, which was a quick and easy fix. Sweet as sugar, Jessica asked about the grumpy guy she met while caroling."

Angela snort-laughs. "I bet she has the voice of an angel when she sings."

"More like an unholy gossip as she announces my private life to the world."

"Yeah, she's a buttinsky, but she had proof." Angela opens pictures on her phone and scrolls to the right one. "Mr.

Tall, fair, gorgeous, and is that a facial scar?" She fans herself and shows a picture of Aaron and me on the porch, begging off the Christmas carolers. A new fault line fractures my heart when I see his handsome face.

Grace points and giggles as I stare at the photo. "You're adorable when you're lovestruck!"

"Stop!" I plead, heat creeping up my face.

Students and parents, drawn by the enticing aroma of cooking meat, file into the room and circle the trays of burgers and hot dogs. Their arrival marks the end of our conversation. Although Divergence Academy promotes community and connection, I don't want my time with Aaron diluted by sharing it with everyone within earshot.

In no time, Elaine dishes up their empty plates with a hearty portion of everything, before declaring, "Private meeting," as she shoos them out.

"Pretend I'm invisible," she insists after the room empties.

Rolling my eyes, I give in. No escape until I talk.

"His name is Aaron Hanson. He's a student's uncle whom I run into on the days when Jeff and I have our extracurricular activities. Jeff's mother forgot to leave my holiday gift, so she had her brother bring it over so I'd have it under the tree for Christmas. The storm got intense, and Aaron admitted he wasn't paying attention when he pulled into the road and rear-ended Craig's tow truck."

"Aww. Craig Bennett—our first year, right? The sixth-grade crush who never stopped falling."

I admit to the truth of Grace's assessment with a nod. I've been honest with Craig about my students and that I categorize them under a special policy, which states that regardless of when they attended D.A., they remain students in my heart. But everyone knows first loves are hard to move past.

"Craig is a good friend. I asked him to drive Aaron home after we knew his car would need a tow, but Craig said he couldn't have passengers."

"Bullshit." Angela smacks the table flat-palmed as she swears. "He didn't want to help the competition."

She and Grace share a knowing look.

"Craig's sweet," Angela sighs. "And so innocent, he didn't realize denying a ride set up a classic romance trope—forced proximity! My favorite."

Grace underlines Angela's statement with a low, feline growl and a swipe of her claws, cracking them up again.

When the mirth passes, I ask, "Are you finished?"

"Honestly, it was chaotic, not romantic." I sigh, uncomfortable downplaying things, but there's too much to do. "Aaron hit his head when he crashed and was bleeding. He should have gone to the hospital, but I handled it. Turns out, I'm a pretty good bedside nurse."

"Ooooh!" Angela rubs her hands together eagerly. "The Hurt/Comfort trope. Did you kiss all his booboos, or just the scars on his soul?"

Oh, bother. My friends' laughter is infectious, though I try not to join in.

My eyes shift from Angela to Grace. They've been as close to me as sisters, and I love them as much as family. I want to tell them how much Aaron meant to me, how he made me feel truly seen and beautiful when he looked my way. But how much do I tell? How much will I lose if I bare it all? Will the Technicolor memories tarnish if they learn how easily I fell in love? Almost like I was halfway there when he showed up at my house. Our shared animosity fueled the passion we discovered, only to realize it was the same ruse we had used to protect our hearts. What about describing how playful Aaron becomes when he frolics with the dogs?

How hard is it to appreciate him if you only know his Monday-to-Friday persona? He's a natural-born teacher, and watching him train three playful puppies and their damaged but resilient mother has been nothing short of brilliant. Would they poopoo the idea because human children are harder to work with?

When I reflect on those days, they feel touched by a golden light, as if removed from normal experience. How do I describe joy that felt so simple? A quote by Kahlil Gibran comes to mind. "Travel and tell no one, live a true love story and tell no one, live happily and tell no one, people ruin beautiful things."

People ruin beautiful things.

Our story and all that occurred between us need to be protected and remain pristine.

I feel free enough to laugh along with Angela and Grace as heaviness ebbs away. Their banter is more than a break from heartache—it's a reminder not to take things too seriously. Just saying Aaron's name out loud has relieved some of the fear around facing what we had and what we lost.

I'm grateful I met Aaron and banked so many memories. We shared many snapshot-in-time moments, and I wouldn't trade any of them. The pain that greets me in the morning and tries to follow me to bed at night is from wanting to relive the magic. But nothing lasts forever. New experiences will overwrite the old, and my recall will turn sweet as I reminisce.

My epiphany releases the tension in my shoulders, grief shifting into cautious optimism. No adventure was ever had by wasting precious moments—or letting them paralyze me. Life is great. It's important to be ready for the next surprise.

We drain the last of our drinks, and Elaine busses them and wipes the table clean like the rest of the kitchen.

"Thanks, Elaine. It was delicious," I speak for the three of us.

"This is easier than what you ladies are doing. Keep up the good work." She unties her apron and hangs it on a hook before leaving us alone.

The doe-eyed expressions on Angela and Grace suggest they want to know more about Aaron. I'm going to disappoint them.

"This was fun," I say, folding the list. "There's not much more to the tale. Aaron came, needed medical help, animals arrived, then he left."

"Hey!" they protest, upset at my summary.

With a look filled with compassion, I explain, "Come on. You know me: lists and work and all kinds of seriousness. The most exciting thing that happened was the number of animals the storm spat out. They kept us busy, busy, busy." With my hands flat on the table, I push up to stand, stronger than ever. "Now come on. Times a wastin'. Let's get back to work."

They call out, begging for more as I make a hasty retreat with private thoughts on Aaron's intense energy, sensuous kisses, and cutting wit effectively guarded.

15

*D*ad and Freddie are due to arrive soon to celebrate a belated Christmas. The silence hit me hard after the volunteers left, so I invited them to an impromptu party to soothe the last of my breakup wounds. At least I think it was a breakup. Whatever we had between us is over. It's time to engage with what matters: authentic relationships.

The house and decorations are back where they belong, returning the construction zone to a home. The place looks festive as I move around, checking the details to ensure a traditional holiday vibe.

Soft music plays in the background. The fire blazes on one side of the room, offset by the lit Christmas tree with gifts underneath. The porcelain tea cups, once my mother's favorites, overflow with candies and nuts. Mismatched yard sale finds, staples of childhood Christmases, are scattered among nests of balsam, glass baubles, and glitter.

Happy reflections uplift my spirits as the scent of turkey fills the air. I can do this 2.0 version of Faith with a heart still broken but growing stronger for the experience. Just as I savor this insight, a knock sounds at the door.

I rush across the floor to answer. "Dad! Freddie! Merry Christmas!"

They drop gift-laden bags at their feet, and we hug each other tight. A deep sense of connection rushes in. The frenzy of their arrival makes the house feel like it's lived in again.

I forgot how a bear hug from my father could wipe any pain away, even if only temporarily. The embrace makes me feel tiny and safe—a welcome shift from the weightiness of loss to feeling loved and worthy, all the good things.

My brother's hugs are more perfunctory, but I cherish them for the emotion behind them.

"Come in, come in," I say, picking up their bags. "What did you bring? These weigh a ton!"

Dad rubs his hands together, excited. "Now that I'm a pet grandfather, lots of toys and treats." Christmas was always his favorite.

"I brought nothing. Coal for you this year," Freddie deadpans.

I roll my eyes at the cliché.

He scans the room. "Is this everyone?"

I hide a smirk and taunt him. "Expecting someone else? Maybe that redhead you've been pining for forever. Still got the hots for Angela, I see."

Freddie reddens to the same shade as my friend's glorious head of hair, shoving past me to avoid the question. "Mind your own business," he warns.

Lifting a finger to the side of his mouth, he says, "Say, Dad mentioned you started collecting pets. Sad, but classic single female behavior for your age."

"Jerk." I punch him in the arm.

"Weirdo," he shoots back.

"That's it. I'm telling." I pull out my phone. "I'm calling

Angela and telling her about the staring, the daydreaming, and how you lo-o-o-ve her from afar."

Freddie grabs my phone and hurls it towards the fire.

Like a Phoenix rising from the ashes, Beth leaps up and catches the phone midair, saving it from burning. Her sense of loyalty makes me braver.

I push Freddie, and he stumbles backwards. "Ha ha! You throw like a girl."

"You'd better pray I choke you like one." Freddie wraps his hands around my neck.

"Enough!" Dad cuts in, breaking up the hold. "No fighting at Christmas."

My brother might be a pest, but it's hard to hold a grudge against the person who can tweak and uplift you without even trying. So, when Dad forces us to hug and make up, we do.

Pounce, being a cat and having no problem owning his feelings about having company, darted back under the bed at the first sign of intruders, but the dogs mill around our feet, sniffing our shoes and whining, eager for attention.

"Who do we have here?" Dad asks. Leaning over, he tries to bend over low enough to pick up a puppy, but his stiff lower back won't let him reach.

"Point to the one you want."

Dad points at Myrrh, and Frank all but leaps into Freddie's waiting arms. I lift Gold, and she sits like a queen in the crook of my elbow as we step into the living room. The sweet moment reminds me that it's the little rituals that bind us.

A few moments later, I resume my hosting duties and offer to take their coats and get them drinks. Both request a beer and shuck off their outerwear, piling it onto my waiting arm as I trade them with Gold.

As I toss the jackets on my bed and head for the kitchen, Dad calls to my retreating back: "You had some repairs done on the house. Looks good. Your Mom would have been thrilled that her love of antique dwellings got passed down."

I answer as I return with cold drinks and some nibbles. "Not planned, but yeah. I'm happy with the result. How did you fare in the storm?"

Beth snuggles close and lays her muzzle on my lap. It looks like love, but it's more about the liver treats hidden in my hand. I dole them out as the guys tell me about the dusting in Connecticut.

"It was no big deal," Dad says. "We're just glad we could make it. We don't see you nearly enough."

I snuggle close to my dad and rest my head on his shoulder. "I miss you too, Dad."

"Blue Christmas," sung by Elvis in the background, shifts the mood and reminds us all of our favorite person, bringing a quiet pause to the room.

Freddie says what we're all thinking, "I wish Mom were here."

Five years have passed since she succumbed to juvenile-onset diabetes, a disease she fought her entire life. Fifty-seven is too young to go, but after Zane passed away, she stopped fighting so hard.

The song finishes, and soon I'm passing around tissues and appetizers; it's left us a bit teary and melancholy. The silence lingers as we indulge in some crackers and cheese after the music and memories have passed.

"Say," says Dad in a falsely cheerful voice. "Did I ever tell you about the time your mother almost wasn't your mother?"

With a queer expression, Freddie says, "Huh? How is that possible?"

Dad grabs a handful of mixed nuts and begins.

"You remember how much your mother loved our house,

right? Redecorating was her passion. When we met, I had to convince her how I was better than every suitor by plying her with elaborate dates, pricey gifts, and lots of flexing muscles. But with that farmhouse, it was love at first sight."

"Aww," I give Dad a squeeze. "Don't feel bad. It was a spectacular house."

"Thanks a lot," Dad quips. "And you're right. I couldn't compete with that antique. I thought we were looking for something more conventional, say a Cape Cod or a colonial. Classic New England, in a nice neighborhood where our future kids could roam and play.

"It was the end of the day, and we'd been in so many houses, they all blurred together. All we wanted was to get back to our apartment, open a bottle of wine, and–" He coughs into his hand. "Let's just say we wanted to get to bed."

"Ew, gross. TMI," says Freddie, blocking his ears with two fingers.

"Let him have his youthful indiscretions," I defend.

"That was your mother!" Dad admonishes, "not an indiscretion." His faraway look is wistful. "Ah, but she was beautiful back then.

"Anyhow, I took a wrong turn, and we ended up lost for an hour. Your Mom was not happy, and things weren't looking good for Valentino here. We argued over stopping and asking for directions. I was all for it, and Mom–" His voice fills with tears. "Well, you know her."

"She depended on her sense of direction, especially when any of us were lost," I impart. She was rather skilled at it, particularly when feeling lost was a result of being beaten up by life. Growing up was manageable because she was always there to guide us. I could use her wisdom now, but instead, I sink into the couch and enjoy Dad's story.

"That she did," Dad agrees.

When the story pauses, Freddie shakes his empty beer bottle. "Anyone need another?" Dad and I decline and ask for a glass of water instead.

While Freddie gathers the drinks, we tussle with the dogs and pass out more treats. By the time Freddie returns, I'm ready for more of the story.

"We hadn't seen another house or car in a while, which is why your mother finally relented and suggested that I stop at the next available dwelling to ask for help. Lo and behold, your childhood home was just around the next bend.

We could hardly see the decrepit Victorian from the street. The brush was so thick, it nearly hid everything. The house looked haunted, and I knew no one would be there to help guide us–nobody living, at any rate.

"Somehow, your mother saw right through it. When we got out of the car, she ran from place to place, pushing the thorny brambles aside to point out all the things she'd pictured when she imagined the perfect place: the post and rail fence, an ancient asparagus bed, and raspberry canes that went on forever.

"'Hank! A barn!' She ran across the lawn, overgrown so it resembled a wheat field, and pushed her way inside. Barely large enough to house a single horse, it had two stalls inside, probably used for ponies or goats. The panes of glass in the windows were crusted with gunk, and she cleaned them off with spit and a tissue before looking out. "'Look! An outhouse,' she cried. "I couldn't believe it. Had we stepped through some portal and gone back in time?"

Dad's last words feel like a slap in the face. Aaron said the same thing when he realized he'd be spending Christmas without electricity and a garage full of chickens. The reminder stings, sending a flush of anger up my neck, but I force myself to shrug it off, hoping no one notices my reaction.

"We stayed until the sun began to set, exploring all the hidden hidey-holes. Mom was no longer angry about being lost. 'This is the place, Hank. This is our new home.'

"Who was I to say no? So, I said yes, but the next morning, I had second thoughts. The house wasn't the most expensive one we looked at, but it cost enough that I'd need the promotion I was in the running for to make the payments. It seemed foolhardy for our first home to be our dream home, and I told her as much over breakfast.

"'What we need is a starter home. Something to build equity with and grow from.' I felt so mature and adult until she stood up from the table and cleared her dishes into the sink. I can see her turning around, so slow, her face so stern.

"'It's that house, or it's nothing,' she said before turning on her heel and leaving the apartment. She was gone all day. To this day, I have no idea where she went, though I suspect she had her sister drive her back to the house to plan the remodel. She spent the next three nights sleeping on the couch and didn't utter a single word to me. She didn't cook. She didn't clean. And Mom wasn't in an amorous mood.

"I went to my dad for advice. He'd been married forty years by then. He must have learned the intricacies of a woman's mind. I just needed to be let in on the secret. He listened with a nod here and there, and when I finished, still optimistic that I'd at least hear that he was on my side, he said, 'Looks like you're going to have to buy that house.'

"That was it. No unraveling the mystery, just 'Buy the house.'

"Point to Mom," says Freddie.

"All the points to Mom. She never had to fight with me

over what she wanted again," Dad admits, with a loving smile.

"Any regrets?" I ask.

"Not one."

"How about any nuggets of wisdom?" Freddie wants to know, I'm sure, so that he can apply it to Angela and his snail-paced wooing approach.

"Don't dig in your heels or believe that results are in yours or anyone else's hands. Life has its way of working things out."

Nodding, I tell him, "I like it. But I'm curious about one thing. How did you and Mom find your way home that night?"

"Oh. Well. We didn't find our way home that night." He smiles and takes a drink of water. "We grabbed some blankets from the trunk and spread them out in the middle of the yard. We made love looking at the stars, and–"

"Please stop," Fredde begs.

"Would you grow up?" I admonish my brother before kicking him in the leg, because I'm his little sister and keeping him in line is my job.

He kicks me back, but the intensity is affection.

"And talking about our future," Dad continues, ignoring our immaturity. "Two weeks later, Mom found out she was pregnant with Freddie, and our happy family began to grow. Life was good, and your Mom is the reason why."

We raise our drinks, and Dad says, "To Mom, the best of us."

"uys. Seriously. Where are we going?" My heels snag on the cobblestones again, frustration simmering beneath my words.

"Try walking like a normal person," Angela huffs, tugging my arm.

"Almost there." Grace's tone is reassuring.

The last place I wanted to spend New Year's was at a party, blindfolded. But my friends claimed a night out would cure heartbreak. They dragged me off the couch and forced me into a dress, insisting I needed a distraction. I disagreed, but now I'm here, heels snagging on cobblestones.

"Aren't surprises fun?"

"Not when they cause an injury." I shoot Grace a look even though I can't see a thing as my ankle threatens to roll.

"Don't be so dramatic." Angela's voice holds no mercy.

My friends claim to care about my post-breakup hermit status, but they don't get it. My couch and comfy clothes are my sanctuary, safe from the sadness and anxiety I feel around others. Lounging is how I heal, not by following their fun. Out here, I just feel exposed and tense.

And is it just me, or is New Year's Eve always brutally cold? People think the holiday is transformative. But January 1 feels like any other cold winter day. A letdown in its predictability: coffee, chores, and prepping for work. Nothing special. Only the end of winter break feels real. Why should tonight be different?

"Three steps, and you've made it!" Cheerleader Grace looks ready to leap for joy.

The slick ground wants to shove me back. I tap the tip of my shoe on each stair to avoid misstepping, since no one else seems concerned with safety.

Angela hits the doorbell and releases her hold on my arm.

I sense her step back as footsteps approach the door.

"Where are you ladies going?" I whisper, shivering.

My friends shout, "See ya!" and, before I can react, run away, leaving me alone on the landing.

"Hey!" I snap at their retreating backs, yanking the silk scarf away. "Don't you dare leave me here!"

The door swings wide. Before I can react, I'm pulled into a hug so heady it outdoes my father's. It feels like my wounds are healed, my ugly parts wiped away. Nothing hurts. Every cell sighs in delight.

Despite myself, my arms wrap around Aaron's midriff and soak up his warmth. He smells of vanilla and peppermint, like a frosted Christmas cookie. It's sheer willpower that stops me from taking a taste.

"I've missed you so much," he whispers into my hair. "Why didn't you call?"

I pull back, breaking the embrace. A pang of loss hits instantly, and a cold regret replaces the warmth. The comfort of intimacy vanishes, replaced by the messier emotions I'd been trying to avoid. I collect myself and tell the pain to buzz off.

"Why would I call you?"

Aaron snickers, all dimples and sparkling eyes. "Who cares, right? You're here now, and nothing else matters."

I'm about to argue when he grabs my hand and pulls me inside.

"It's freezing out. Let's get you a warm drink, and I'll show you my surprise."

"I've had enough surprises for one night."

My words fall on deaf ears.

Resigned, I unwind my scarf and remove my coat, handing them over to be hung on the brass coat rack, a move he makes look deceptively domestic.

As usual, I look up. The foyer's leaded glass dome isn't fussy, but its size makes up for the lack of color. On a regular day, I like to run my fingers over the smooth mahogany table, which reflects the image on its shiny surface, but tonight's party means no stalling.

"Where's the booze?" I'd rather know why I'm here, but first things and some liquid courage first.

With a crook of a finger over his shoulder, Aaron leads me into the kitchen. I follow, not sure what to expect after my friends abandoned me.

No other guests seem to be here. Usually, the kitchen is packed, to most hosts' dismay. Tonight, the bright, empty room reminds me that this house is unlike mine and that this man is different from me. I should have known better that a contemporary guy and an old-fashioned girl would be doomed from the start. I push aside the question's sadness by wondering if guests are exploring other rooms.

He places an oversized mug in my hands. Steam rises from the top, overflowing with whipped cream and chocolate shavings.

I lick foam off my finger; the drink is unmistakably homemade.

After blowing away whipped cream, I sip. "Mmm." Why does this man do everything well? His only flaw: he's not into me.

"Good, huh?" He leans against the stove, arms crossed. "I made the cocoa from scratch: maple syrup, creme de menthe, Irish cream, and bourbon. Stir with a peppermint cinnamon stick, and you have Addled by Aaron, the perfect party drink."

He reaches over and wipes stray foam from my lip.

"I wanted that." I swipe at my lip, glaring.

"Too late for that, and for this too." He presses his warm, chocolate-flavored lips against mine.

Oh, this! This is what I've missed. For these kisses, I would trade my pride. I sink into his strong arms as he intensifies the kiss. His lips move over mine, slick and needy, as my tongue seeks his to tangle together and mimic what the rest of my body wishes for.

Breaking the kiss before my hunger is sated, he claims, "I've missed you, Faith."

Snapped back at the loss of his lips on mine, shame rushes over me. I realize how quickly I slip into our patterns. Am I mistaking a game for love? Or is it just weakness? A need so sharp I'll reopen the wound for another taste of pain. This can't go on.

I back away so quickly that I hit the pot handle, which is still resting on the hot burner.

"Careful." He reaches around me and saves it from toppling, preventing the remaining liquid from spilling onto the tile floor. He rights the pot and turns off the burner.

"Now. Where were we?" He moves in close, tilting his head down for another kiss.

The near miss has me thinking rationally again. I lash out, gesturing and using air quotes: "'We' were about to tell me what's going on. 'We' were going to explain why 'we' left and never looked back. 'We' were ready to tell us why 'we' pretended to care when 'we' didn't." My voice cracks on the last, but I clear the pain and make one final statement. "We were going to figure out how I can keep working with Jeff, even if it means seeing you and breaking my heart over and over."

By the end of my rant, pain chokes me, and a single tear falls. Confident, capable Faith is gone, replaced by someone lost and exposed. Discomfort churns in my gut like the now-bitter cocktail.

Resting a hand over my chest, I take a deep breath and will myself to relax. I remind myself, as I tell my students: everything passes, not just the good, not only spring. Winter ends, and pain lessens. *I'm okay.*

Opening my eyes, I find him watching me. The eleven lines between his brows furrow so tightly together that they create a monobrow.

"Where is this coming from?"

The situation feels hopeless. Every attempt at conversation this week only reminded me how much separates us, intensifying my heaviness and regret. My friends' optimism now feels naive, and I'm angry with myself for holding on to hope. Desperation to escape builds fast; I set the mug in the sink and run water over my shaky fingers, trying to wash away the sticky traces of fear.

"I gotta go." I rush to the door and grab my coat and scarf without pausing to put them on, but I'm not fast enough to exit before Aaron grabs my wrist.

"Please don't go. I think there's been a misunderstanding."

17

*E*xhausted from the chaos of recent weeks, I can't fight any longer. I collapse into a chair, hugging my coat for warmth and safety. My chest aches with vulnerability.

He crouches in front of me. My body remains rigid and tense in the chair. When I don't reply, he scrutinizes my face, reading my frown as a willingness to listen.

"You seemed thrown when I asked why you didn't call. Didn't you get my note?"

My head lifts in surprise. "What note?"

"The note I gave Craig," Aaron explains. "He rushed me out, so I barely said goodbye. I left my number and invited you over for New Year's Eve. I had something for you. I hoped reaching out to the school would help—" He pauses when my eyes narrow.

Frustrated, I throw up my arms. My voice hardens. "Cut the crap. I know your sister lives outside the intake area. You've been lying. For what it's worth, you're not the first." My pitch makes him flinch, and I lower my voice. "Jeff's a good kid; he shouldn't pay for your schemes."

"Thank you," he says, humbler than I expected. "Rachel hated the manipulation. I thought it was for Jeff's good. We should've just asked for a waiver."

"Hold up. The school doesn't offer waivers, and you're not in the clear. I'll recuse myself and present your case to the board. Lucky for you, they're softer than me, so don't panic."

Relieved, he reaches for my hand, still grasping my coat in a vise grip. I loosen it into his warm palm.

"We're grateful for any help and forgiveness." He's not just talking about Rachel and Jeff anymore.

"You mentioned a note."

"Yes!" His relief is obvious. "Craig said he'd give it to you right away. He mentioned your house was the cleanup headquarters and that he was on the crew. With cell service still spotty, that seemed the quickest way to contact you. I wanted to thank you for being my nurse, and get help from the committee so I could finish the surprise before you returned to work."

His story sounds truthful, so I shrug off Craig's omission. "Wouldn't be the first time his crush distracted him. The note's probably still in his pocket. But why did my friends bring me here, blindfolded?"

He raises his hands, looking surprised. "I'm innocent! The blindfold was Angela and Grace's idea. When I went to school after no response about getting on the fix-it list, your friends recognized me from a photo. They pulled me into the principal's office, said it was about paperwork, and then locked the door. You're not the only one who got kidnapped."

I tilt my head, realizing Angela and Grace are getting organized with their schemes.

Rising, he begins to pace, recounting the ordeal. "After an intense twenty-question session, they concocted a plan to get you over here on New Year's to celebrate. I didn't ask why. Agreeing seemed the fastest way to get you here and let me leave without them demanding ransom."

I picture the scene: Angela, with her oversized red glasses that shouldn't work with her hair color but do, perched on her nose, pins Aaron in a chair with one hand on his shoulder and the other wielding a clipboard of instructions. I imagine Grace playing "good cop", offering coffee and translating Angela's threats as viable options. A snicker slips out.

Aaron leans over me, hands on his hips, grinning. "You think this is funny?"

"It's hilarious." Laughter spills out.

Aaron grabs my arms and pulls me close.

I'm not sure what he's planning to make me stop laughing, but the sparkle in his eyes makes me think I'll enjoy it.

"Don't you know me? Put a project in front of me, and I get it done. Sometimes at the expense of everything else. Don't take it personally. I'm sure a smart lady like you could learn how to make the tendency work in her favor."

I play obtuse. "I could...but, why should I?"

He turns serious. "Don't play with my feelings, Faith. I couldn't stand it if you didn't love me. Anyone but you."

His words catch me off guard. But I realize I feel the same. Loving someone means risking pain, and I almost flinch from the weight of it.

"You love me? For real?"

"Yes, Faith Quinn, I love you, with all my heart."

"Since when?"

"Since you knocked on my front door and said, 'Can Jeff come out and play,' like the nerdiest girl on the playground."

"I didn't say that!" I smack his arm. *Did I? Is that why he calls me Jeff's playmate?*

"You did say that." He draws a big X over his heart. "You said using the phrase made you appear as a friend rather than an authority figure, which put the students at case. 'Sets them up for success!' you stated with a dorky, theatrical flip of your arm."

Shoot! I do say that. Still, he's not off the hook entirely. "Hey! Offended."

He wears an innocent look. "What?"

"You said I was a nerd, not a dork."

"What's the difference?"

"Nerds are smart and can be hot, especially when they remove their glasses and let their hair down. Think sophisticated librarians and girls who can dominate in Fortnite. The hard biological truth about dorks is you can't be cool if you mend your glasses with tape and use pencil holders in shirt pockets. Their hair doesn't flow as much as it appears greasy and matted."

He looks skeptical. "How do you know these distinctions?"

"Simple." I adopt a virtuous mien. "I'm a teacher. It's my job."

"Glad to see where my tax dollars are going."

We don't accept government funding," I reply, repeating a common retort.

"Can we get back to the point? Your memory stinks, and I have something to show you." He softens his words by placing a tender kiss on the tip of my nose.

"Fine." I raise a fist. "But call me a dork again."

He takes my fist and kisses the knuckles. "You are the hottest nerd. Thanks for clarifying. Forgiven?"

Hope and caution battle as we step into this new territory. I cling to my defensive ways. "Depends. What's my surprise?"

Without a word, he leads me by the hand toward the back of the house. We pass through the kitchen, and he pauses to swing open a door to the garage. He flips a switch, illuminating the space as we descend a short flight of stairs. Aaron appears too polished to be handy, yet the array of power tools on the workbench and neatly arranged on pegboards shows where he spends his free time.

He stops us in front of a large object hidden underneath a cloth tarp. Aaron grabs one corner of the tarp and pulls it back, then gestures for me to hold the other side and help reveal what's underneath.

The sturdy wooden box gleams under the fluorescent lights. I circle it, noting sliding windows on three sides and a Dutch door. Dropping to my knees, I peer inside at plaster walls and a ceiling painted sky blue. The windows and doors are framed in white, and the floor is tiled in black-and-white mosaic. Cheerful linen valances, trimmed with whimsical red fire hydrants, add a touch of brightness to the space. In the center sits a thick, canvas-covered bed inviting rest. Steel dog bowls, mounted on metal rings, complete the design.

Propping myself up on a forearm against the comfortable bed, I look through the back window at Aaron, who stands outside, staring in to gauge my reaction.

"What a beautifully crafted dog house! You built this?"

"Yup. I was afraid I wouldn't have the time when no one from the cleanup committee got in touch. But Rachel and I were lucky with a few broken windows, one cracked water pipe, and tons of leaves to rake between us.

"Jeff raked like a child possessed when he heard he'd get $50 to spend any way he wanted for his efforts."

"Let me guess. He bought a terrarium."

"A fancy glass one he's storing iguana snacks in."

The kid collects terrariums of all shapes and sizes, most

filled with plastic plants, and some are used to raise caterpillars or house fireflies, which serve as nightlights on occasion.

"Ew. How is Lester?"

"Boring, but Jeff watches him for hours. Better than video games, I suppose."

Aaron squeezes into the doghouse until we're face-to-face, and the scene shifts from workspace to cozy retreat.

"This took a lot of work. Beth and the pups will love it. Thank you." The kiss we share shows my appreciation, too.

"I wanted to build two so they wouldn't feel squeezed in, but we have time. They're still small.

"How did they do at the vet?"

"As you'd expect. Beth was stoic, and the pups were squirmy and sweet. They love shots now because the vet tech dispensed a strip of canned cheese with every pinch.

"I'm sorry you didn't get any help. I'll talk to him and reiterate the importance of the community. Every member. Not just the ones he deems unthreatening."

"I'd be jealous, too, if the shoe were on the other foot. You're a special lady."

I kiss him three times for the compliment before an alarm on his phone breaks the spell.

"Five minutes." He flips the screen towards me. 11:55. "Ready to ring in the new year?"

He sits up, opens a hidden cupboard over the door, and pulls out a bottle of cold champagne and matching champagne flutes. Popping out the cork, he pours us each a glass. With a crisp clink, we toast to the year gone by, which brought us so much.

"You realize we're celebrating in a dog house."

"Unplanned, but appropriate. Based on getting to know each other these past weeks and your guilty-until-proven-innocent approach to relationships, I'd better get used to the place."

"Beth will love it."

"Just Beth?"

"No. Myrrh seems to favor you, too."

Aaron admonishes me with a raised eyebrow. "Faith..."

It's time to swallow my fears, and I admit, "I love you, Aaron Hanson. I'll learn to see the real you, not just Aaron the Arrogant."

"It would stand to reason, future bride," he says, clinking his glass against mine again before taking a sip.

Shocked at his words, my hands shake hard enough for the champagne to spill over the edges.

As another phone alarm goes off, Aaron raises his glass for a toast that goes unmet. "Happy New Year!"

"B-b-bride?" I struggle to say.

"Wedding, honeymoon, babies, all of it." He acts like none of those things is a big deal.

Someone has been doing a lot of planning behind my back, and it is taking me a minute to catch up.

"We'll live here and use your place when we feel like roughing it."

"Hey." I defend my modest abode. "It's a nice place."

Classic. He pretends not to hear anything he disagrees with. "Raise our kids to be smart like their mom, crafty like their dad, and lovable like their fur siblings. What do you say?"

He's got me warming to the idea of him, us, and all the rest. I shrug my shoulder, trying out his whimsical attitude. "Can we move in tonight?"

"I'll drink to that."

We toast and drain our glasses before he swoops me into

his arms and lays us back on the dog bed, kissing me sense-less. With so much to gain, we lose ourselves in the cele-bration.

The End

AFTERWORD

I hope you enjoyed reading O Holy Heck! Stranded for Christmas. Please consider leaving a review on Amazon and share your thoughts with others.

Please stay in touch by signing up for my monthly newsletter at www.kathleenpendoley.com and following me on Bookbub and Amazon for information about new releases, blog posts, and more.

ACKNOWLEDGMENTS

Nine books in, and I've been remiss in thanking God, from whom all things derive. It's helpful to know someone is in charge because I've lost any sense of direction.

Thank you so much, Donna D, for taking part in the "Choose the MFC Name" competition. I had "Faith," my name choice wouldn't make it to print.

I'm grateful to my loyal and steadfast sister, Mary Kendzierski, and everyone at the Inn at Ellis River for selling my books and believing in my dream, even when I'm about to give up.

As always, thank you to my husband. In thirty-plus years, so many things can (and do) go wrong, but so much goes right.

Truly, the best part of writing is having readers. I offer my deepest gratitude to everyone who found my book and enjoyed it—thank you!

ALSO BY KATHLEEN PENDOLEY

Novels

Trail of the Heart

Confidence Quest - Sequel to *Trail of the Heart*

Bryant Brothers Novella Series

Beachy Keen Book 1

The Cake Maker's Dog Book 2

Glitter and Grief Book 3

A Nautical Twist Book 4

Holiday novella

Broke By Christmas